THE SHOUTING WIND

"Good God, I'm not wearing those," Felicity protested, holding up a pair of knee-length blue knickers. "What are they made of, old barrage ballooons?"

Kay collected together her bagful of blue-grey tunic and skirt, shirt and collar, lisle stockings, cap, underwear, belt, tie and black Oxford shoes. Within minutes whe was looking at her unrecognisable self in the mirror, neatly buttoned and belted, topped by a blue peaked cap. She looked in every respect the correctly turned out servicewoman.

It was both exciting and daunting. She was impressed by the smartness of the small figure in the glass, but for the first time she felt real qualms at giving up her civilian status. She was not an individual any more. She was 579127 ACW Leary, K., about to be trained to follow orders unquestioningly.

Forthcoming titles in The Shouting Wind *trilogy*

The Cliff Path
A Fear of Heights

Other books by the same author

Some Other War
The Wearing of the Green
The Kind Ghosts

THE
SHOUTING WIND

Linda Newbery

Lions
An *Imprint of* HarperCollins*Publishers*

First published in Great Britain in Lions in 1995
Lions is an imprint of CollinsChildren'sBooks,
a division of HarperCollins Publishers Ltd,
77-85 Fulham Palace Road,
Hammersmith, London W6 8JB

1 3 5 7 9 8 6 4 2

Printed and bound in Great Britain
by HarperCollins Manufacturing Ltd, Glasgow

0 00 674764 7

Acknowledgements

I would not have been able to write this book without considerable help with background details from the following people and organisations, whom I would like to thank.

Pip Beck, author of *A WAAF in Bomber Command*, published by Goodalls, answered my questions, lent me various books and papers, and very kindly allowed me to base the *Darky* incident in the fifth chapter on an incident which she experienced at RAF Waddington and which she has described in her autobiographical book.

The staff of the Battle of Britain Memorial Flight at RAF Coningsby kindly allowed me the privilege of boarding the Lancaster of the flight, one of only two in the world still in flying condition.

The Archive and Musuem department of the British Red Cross provided details of how information was sent to relatives of aircrew who were prisoners-of-war in Germany.

My mother-in-law, Peggy Arrowsmith, told me about her experiences of service life, and her post-war occupation suggested the ending for this novel. I am grateful to both her and my husband for their comments on the first draft.

Particular thanks are due to my father, who flew in Lancasters as a navigator during the war, for his help and encouragement with this and my other books.

Windersby, Bardwell and the Birmingham training depot are fictitious, although all the flying operations I have mentioned did take place as described.

The title of this book is a phrase from the sonnet "High Flight" by Pilot Officer G. Magee of the Royal Canadian Air Force, killed December 11th 1941.

CONTENTS

Prologue

TAMSIN

"*T*his junction," Jim said. "The one for Lincoln."

Tamsin slowed down, flicked the indicator upwards and changed gear carefully. She was conscious of Jim watching her, exacting and critical, all the time she was driving. She needed the practice, but sometimes wished she didn't need his approval so badly. She thought she had got over that; but perhaps she never would. And for all his remoteness at times, he had understood at once why she wanted to make the journey today, and what she wanted to find.

She negotiated the junction, concentrating hard, and they left behind the busy A1 with its Little Chefs and cone-strewn contraflows. They were on a country road now. This was more like the scenery Nan would have known fifty years ago: hedgerows, fields of ripening barley, a sprawling stone village decked with bunting for a fête. A heat-haze shimmered over the road surface. The sky was a clear, almost burning blue, streaked with cirrus:

a big sky, as people always said of East Anglia. A vast, arching bowl of blue, a flying sky. Had the sun shone like this for Nan, the first time she'd approached? In a transport bus, probably; but then she'd have come by train as far as Lincoln, so she'd have come from the opposite direction . . . For a moment she imagined them meeting at the gates, converging from their different halves of the century. What would Nan-then think of me-now, she wondered, with all the privileges she'd never have dreamed of? A place at university, a car to drive about in (even if it's Jim's, not mine); and most of all, freedom from the threat of war, as far as that can ever be guaranteed . . .

"Not much further now.' Jim looked up from his road atlas to point at an AA sign at the junction ahead: Air Day, RAF Windersby.

"It doesn't seem too busy after all," Tamsin said, "considering the weather."

Half a mile out of the village they came to a halt behind a queue of traffic. AA signs directed coaches one way, cars another; looking across the fields to her right, Tamsin saw glittering acres of car windscreens, aircraft hangars, a control tower. Cadets in army camouflage waved the cars on down a narrow track and on to a grass strip bordering the runway.

Tamsin parked – not quite straight; Jim made no comment, although she saw him noticing – and they got out of the car, stretching stiff legs. It was going to be very hot; the sun was already beating down fiercely over the treeless airfield. Tamsin felt herself beginning to relax into the freedom of a summer Saturday and at the same time tensing with expectation. She put on a wide-brimmed hat, rolled her sleeves down and checked that the car doors were locked.

"Let's get a programme first," Jim said, "then a drink."

He took Tamsin's hand as they walked down the concrete track towards the main buildings, where most of the spectators were congregating. Tamsin curled her fingers round his and looked around at the airfield, trying to blot the crowds and the candy-floss stalls and the hot-dog vans from her vision. There was a large ivy-clad building by what seemed to be the main entrance; surely that must have been there then? And the hangars, perhaps they dated back to the war? But the milling crowds intruded, and the past obstinately refused to superimpose itself on the present. Jim detached himself to sort coins from his pocket and went over to a programme stall, while she tried to picture groups of newly trained WAAF reporting to the guard-room. Her imagination would supply only the image of a black-and-white photograph from Nan's album, rows of smiling young women with names like Pearl and Joyce and Dot, in their smart uniforms and lace-up shoes . . .

Jim slid an arm round her shoulders. "Come on! Standing there daydreaming . . . I've got a programme. The display starts in ten minutes. I'd like to look at that fighter before that."

He led her towards a roped-off aircraft with its cockpit yawning open like the mouth of a great white shark, revealing a bewildering array of electronic indicators. A young pilot in flying overalls stood by the ropes facing an interested crowd. Jim was fascinated, Tamsin could see, envying the pilot. A loud-voiced boy of about twelve elbowed past Tamsin, wearing a T-shirt with the slogan *Desert Storm Victory*, as if claiming some personal credit. The Gulf War had been uncomfortably like an adventure watched on TV, she remembered; a computer game, with smart weapons and surgical strikes and state-of-the-art military technology. Not like Nan's war, the ordinary people's war . . .

Jim pulled at her arm, as excited as a schoolboy. "It's nearly time for the display to start. It's a Harrier first. Let's go over by the runway."

Tamsin looked over the level grass where once Lancaster bombers had waited for take-off. She had come here to see the Lancaster and the Spitfires and the airfield itself; modern aircraft meant nothing to her. But the roar of jet engines demanded all attention, and when the arrow-shape of the Harrier fighter skimmed low overhead, the sound lagging seconds behind, she was held mesmerised in spite of herself. A few moments ago she had been thinking that awe of military might was a male characteristic, but she found herself thrilling to the sky-splitting roar and the aerial gymnastics. The streamlined fighter flipped on to its side, banked low in a wide circuit, then returned to hover – hover! – almost over the VIP stand, deafening the spectators, before speeding away again, powered through the air like a supersonic dart. If she could have spoken to Jim with any hope of being heard, she'd have said, "How is it that humans can design a plane like that, but not work out how to feed the world or repair the ozone layer?" But her thoughts veered as abruptly as the Harrier and she was lost in envy of the pilot; it must be like riding a thorough-bred, with an extra dimension thrown in, the whole sky for your racecourse . . . Beside her, Jim stood with a hand up against the sun, his body tensed as if he were imagining the same thing. If we'd lived fifty years ago, Tamsin thought, he'd be flying a Spitfire or a Lancaster, and I'd be doing my war-work and waiting for news of him, waiting for him to be shot down.

Grateful because she did not have to, she slipped her arm through his in a rush of affection, and he looked down at her and said something she could not hear. The Harrier finished its display, waggling its wings in farewell as it banked low over the horizon, and there was a brief pause over the crowd, the sort of stunned pause that follows a play or a concerto just before the first person starts clapping, a silent acknowledgement of seeing or hearing something exceptional. Tamsin's eardrums slowly returned to normal, and the public address system announced that the next item would be an aerobatics display by matching biplanes.

Jim shook his head vigorously like a dog clearing its ears of water, and said, "It was worth coming just for that. Incredible, wasn't it?"

"I wonder what Nan would say if she were here? I bet the Lancaster and Spitfires would be the only things she'd recognise.'

"Your grandad was based here as well, wasn't he?"

Tamsin nodded. "They met here."

It was always her grandmother she thought of, though: Kay − Leary, her surname would have been then − in her new WAAF uniform, barely eighteen, not even as old as Tamsin was now; a small, determined figure taking her part in the war which was to dominate her young adult years and affect the rest of her life. It must have been a bit like starting university, Tamsin thought, thinking of last October: she was like me, all on her own, not knowing anyone, wondering who she'd meet. Not knowing whether she would cope.

"It's odd, isn't it," Tamsin said, "how people of the war generation often talk about it as if it were the best time of their life. Or – well, the most memorable, as if nothing since has been quite the same. Like Nan and Grandad. Like your grandad, going to all those reunions. Even though it must have been terrible as well."

"I don't think it's odd at all," Jim said, and began to explain why not. Tamsin only half listened. Her thoughts lingered on the phrase she had almost used: *It was the best of times, it was the worst of times*. Perhaps Nan would have known what that meant.

PART ONE:
1943

ACW Leary K.

*T*he open window behind Kay looked over a green swell of hillside, a wide river with a stony bed, and paddocks where sleek brood mares and yearlings grazed in the dusk. Although Kay would soon be leaving the Wicklow Hills for home in bomb-damaged London, she was not looking out at the tranquil evening but at the wall opposite. The attic of the large farm cottage was half cleared, Uncle Jack having had the idea of turning it into an extra sitting-room for his two daughters; at present, a camp bed, a faded sofa and a hanger-rail occupied one end of the long, sloping-eaved room, while the other end was filled with packing cases, cardboard boxes and assorted junk. One of the plaster wall-ends was hung with four framed oil paintings, and it was these which absorbed

Kay's attention until the tread of boots on the ladder from the landing below sent her to the hatchway.

"Tea-tray coming up," Uncle Jack's cheerful voice announced. "One of your last cups of tea as a civilian, so enjoy it. If the catering in the WAAF is anything like I remember in the army, they don't even call it tea till you can stand a spoon up in it."

Kay knelt down by the hatch and reached down with both arms for the tea-tray. There were two cups of tea, and a plate of biscuits. Uncle Jack, relieved of the tray, clomped the rest of the way up and looked at Kay enquiringly.

"I was just having a last look at the paintings," she said.

"I thought you might be." Jack took his cup of tea and a biscuit, and sat down on the sofa. He smelled comfortably of horses and tweed.

"It seems stupid, doesn't it – my father's paintings safe here in Ireland while Mum's stayed on in London through the Blitz?" Kay remarked. "Anyone would think she cared more about them than about her own life."

"I suppose she does, in a way," Uncle Jack said, although Kay had not really been serious. "We've asked her enough times to come over here, even if it was only for a holiday, but I always knew she wouldn't, not Alice. It wouldn't suit her to get away while other people had no choice but to stick it out. It was the thought of your father's paintings being smashed to pieces by the Luftwaffe that really worried her."

"Poor Mum," Kay said. "One war ought to be enough for anyone's lifetime."

"Yes," Jack said emphatically.

Kay guessed that he was thinking of his own experience as well as her mother's, his twin sister. He had been in the army from the second year of the Great War, and had spent some time in hospital after being gassed. After the war, he had made a new life at the stud farm in County Wicklow; he was happily married to Aunt Sarah, with an adopted son, and two daughters of their own. Even so, the current war threatened his happiness. As well as Alice stubbornly remaining in the East End of London, Jack had his son to worry about: Stephen, in spite of having spent nearly all his life in Ireland, had insisted on going to England to join the RAF, and was training as a pilot.

"I keep thinking how different things might be now," Kay said, "if my father hadn't been killed. We'd be living in Dublin, all three of us, and none of us need be involved with the war at all."

Jack said, "Stephen needn't have been involved, and yet he chose to be. The what-ifs and the if-onlys, they get you down if you let them."

Kay wasn't sure she followed his point, and then realised that he was referring to some future *if-only*, if something happened to Stephen. Stephen wanted to be a fighter pilot. Her stomach knotted when she thought of what he might be doing in a few weeks' time, and she felt a wrench of pity for Uncle Jack; it must be awful to be out of the war, waiting for news, unable to influence events. At least when she became a WAAF she'd be involved, doing something useful. Since enlisting a month ago, she had feared that the RAF didn't want her, or had forgotten about her; now a letter had come from her mother at home saying that details had arrived from the Air Ministry, and that Kay was to report for duties early next week. The waiting was nearly over.

Kay looked across at her father's self-portrait, one of the most precious of the evacuated paintings. The father she had never known gazed back at her. She had grown up with this image, which her mother treated with iconic reverence. Over the years Kay had watched her father apparently growing younger as the difference between her age and his narrowed. Patrick Leary had died at the age of twenty-nine, twelve years older than Kay was now. If he had lived he would have been a little older than Uncle Jack and her mother, well into his forties. But his premature death meant that he would always be twenty-nine, looking out of his picture frame with an expression of puzzled introspection.

Kay knew from her mother's photographs that he had not flattered himself in the painting. He had been an attractive man, not conventionally handsome, perhaps, but with a broad, strong-boned face dominated by deep-set brown eyes and dark brows. Kay did not think she resembled him at all, having inherited her mother's hazel eyes and fragile appearance, so that it was sometimes difficult to convince herself that she was actually related to the man in the painting, familiar though he was. She thought that perhaps the other pictures revealed more of his personality: the landscapes of the Wicklow Hills, which he had loved, and of the remoter parts of Ireland he had visited with Alice during their brief marriage. The gunman who had fired the fatal shot in the troubled Ireland of the 'twenties had robbed Alice of a husband, Kay of a father, and Patrick of his future, all in one mistaken instant.

"I suppose he'd be a famous artist by now if he'd lived," Jack said, following her gaze. "Exhibiting at the smart galleries in Dublin."

"Now you're starting on the if-onlys," Kay said. She finished her tea. "I'd better start packing."

Jack stood up and brushed biscuit crumbs from his tweed jacket. "All right then, Aircraftwoman Leary. I'll leave you to get on with it."

When Kay got back to the London flat, the first thing she saw was the buff Air Ministry envelope with the joining-up details in it, propped in front of the wireless on the mantelpiece. She had taken the first letter, the one confirming her acceptance, to Ireland with her. She had looked at it whenever she doubted that she really was going to be a WAAF; the peaty hills and remote valleys she had explored on one of Uncle Jack's quieter horses had seemed continents away from crowded training camps and operational airfields. Soon it would be the other way round: the RAF would be the reality, the Wicklow Hills a distant dream.

It still gave her a surprise to see herself addressed as ACW Leary, K. She picked up the letter, still feeling bad about the way she had broken the news to Alice. She had said nothing about her visit to the recruiting office, nothing at all until the first letter had come. She had remained silent partly through doubt that the Women's Auxiliary Air Force would accept her, and partly because she knew that Alice would not like it.

"But why the WAAF?" had been Alice's first question.

Kay had looked at her mother uncertainly, all her reasons evaporating. Alice was leaning back in an armchair, her face tired and drawn. She always looked tired, because she would have considered any day wasted which didn't end in exhaustion. She worked every day at an East End children's clinic and helped at a local rest centre in the evenings and at weekends. Kay, who had been evacuated to Malvern with her school since the beginning of the Blitz, sometimes felt as if she had run away, leaving Alice to cope alone.

"Well, I—"

What were her reasons? She wasn't at all sure they were creditable.

"It's better than working in munitions," she said.

"I didn't mean that. I meant, what's the attraction of the air force, in particular?"

"I suppose because it's new and different," Kay said. "A lot of the jobs for women haven't changed much since the last war – jobs like nursing or driving an ambulance. The WAAF is different. And Mr Churchill said that only the air force can win the war."

"Hmm." Alice did not look convinced, but she said no more. Kay had the feeling that her mother would have preferred her to be a nurse or an ambulance driver. Kay understood, up to a point: Alice, a member of the Peace Pledge

Union, thought that women in wartime should carry out humanitarian duties, not contribute in any way to the conflict. Alice had been a nurse throughout most of the Great War and was a confirmed pacifist as a result of her experiences. But this is my life, and my generation's war, Kay thought obstinately; I've got to make my own decisions.

"I can't just stay at home, when the services are recruiting girls my age," she said. "You wouldn't have done. You *didn't*."

"I don't expect you to stay at home," her mother said. "Of course you want to do something worthwhile. But last time we discussed it you were talking about being a Land Girl."

"Yes, but that was before . . ." Kay's voice trailed off. Before what? Before she had seen Stephen in his air force uniform? Before she had seen the posters urging young women to *Serve in the WAAF with the Men who Fly*? Before she had started to fancy herself pushing markers in an Operations Room, like a croupier in a casino, attracting the glances of handsome off-duty pilots?

"Before what?" Alice asked.

"Before I really thought about it," Kay finished lamely. She could not explain that the air force offered a glamour and excitement which could not be matched by nursing or cooking or farming, nor even by the other women's services. "Most parents would be *proud* of their daughter for joining the WAAF," she added, a little resentfully. "Mary Edwards' parents could hardly wait to see her in uniform and have her photo on the piano for everyone to admire." The trouble with Mum, she thought, is that everything's got to be so thoroughly moral.

"Yes, I know they would," Alice said. "Well, I'm sorry. I know you're doing what you think best."

Kay was not much placated by this but tried not to show it, and soon Alice relented enough to ask her where she had gone to enlist and what they had asked at the interview. They had talked about war work before; Kay's eighteenth birthday was only a few months away, and she would be conscripted if she did not enlist voluntarily. Now that her Higher examinations were behind her, Kay had seen no reason not to join up immediately instead of waiting until September. If it hadn't been for the war, her mother would have wanted her to apply for a university place; but Kay could hardly remember a time when there hadn't been war. *Before the war* was a hazy, distant time, belonging to her childhood. Yet she could remember quite clearly when the war had become real to her, during the Blitz: one morning on her walk to school she came upon the smashed remnants of a pair of bombed houses, and had stood among the crowd which had gathered morbidly to watch firemen searching through the rubble. Horrified, Kay had seen upper floors sliding and tipping, a mirror hanging drunkenly askew, flowered bedroom wallpaper exposed as if the house were a parcel ripped open by greedy hands, and bricks and mortar were no more substantial than brown paper and string. There was a smell of gas and dust and cordite, and a broken water pipe spilled its contents into the gutter. This was war, then: homes destroyed without warning, frail human bodies torn to pieces in the ferocity of an explosion, or slowly crushed to death in the rubble. And then an adult hand grasped Kay's shoulder and drew her aside, and a voice told her to get along to school and not to get in the way.

Not getting in the way seemed to be a child's first duty. Soon after the bombing started, the whole school had been evacuated to Malvern. Kay could not see the point of it: how was she expected to concentrate on her lessons when she was obsessed by a fear that something would happen to her mother? Why was her mother so obstinate, insisting on staying in London when she didn't have to? Kay was almost angry with her. Why did Alice's sense of duty always have to come before everything else?

Now Kay's school days were over, and she

and her mother were at odds again: politely, and covertly, but still at odds. It was Kay's last evening at home, and she wanted it to go smoothly. She had queued at the fish shop to buy herrings, fish being one of the few foodstuffs which was not rationed, and she had hoarded some sugar to make a fruit crumble for a special supper. Having wanted so much to join the WAAF, she now wished she was staying at home with her mother: the possible demands of service life suddenly began to seem quite terrifying. What would be required of her; would she be up to it? Where would she be sent? Supposing she made some dreadful mistake? Almost as bad was the thought of leaving her mother alone to face the difficulties of London life alone. The worst of the raids seemed to be over, but who could tell when they would resume?

It was partly because Alice had stoically faced the worst of the Blitz, and tended the victims, that Kay found her position illogical. Being a pacifist was all very well, but what use was it in the present situation? What were you supposed to do – sit back on your principles while Hitler invaded? Surely working at a fighter base was more useful? She tried not to think of the possibility that she might not end up at a fighter base. That was what she had joined up for.

There was a miaowing at the balcony window and a cat pressed itself sinuously against the taped glass, attracted by the smell of fish through the open fanlight. Kay opened the window and let the cat in. It was a small black female, found by Alice as a bedraggled and terrified stray in a bombed-out house. Now she was sleek and well-groomed, with the smugness of a cared-for cat. Kay picked her off the draining board and hugged her, her anxious feelings soothed by the warmth of fur and the vibration of the purring body. It almost frightened her, the unexpected rush of love she felt for this cat. Sometimes it was easier to demonstrate love for animals than for people.

At least Alice would have some company at home. Kay put the trilling creature down on the floor and washed her hands before taking what was left of their cheese ration out of the pantry. It would have made things easier if there had been more of a family than just herself and Alice. Kay wondered what her father would have said about her joining up: she often found herself having imaginary conversations with him, although she could not conjure his voice. He had had a deep voice, Alice had told her, with the Dublin accent he had never lost in spite of spending most of his youth in England. Sometimes when Alice talked about him she sounded like a girl again, her eyes distant as if she could see him. She had been desperately unlucky, Kay knew, losing both her loves: first a fiancé killed in the first war, and then Patrick, who had died without knowing he had fathered a daughter.

Kay had always known how much the Great War and its aftermath had dominated Alice's life. At the outbreak of war in 1914, Alice had been just eighteen, two months older than Kay was now. Kay washed the herrings carefully and then rummaged in the drawer for a sharp knife, wondering whether her own future would be shaped by events completely beyond her control. The cat twined itself around her ankles, hoping for fish heads.

BEST BLUE

*T*he train was hot and crowded, smelling of dust and cigarette smoke and stale air. Kay looked out at the East Midlands landscape. Progress was erratic, so that sometimes the cornfields and woods sped by, allowing her to play her childhood game of mentally jumping the hedges and gates on horseback, and sometimes giving her time for prolonged study of clinker, nettles and willowherb in a cutting, while the train waited interminably and the other passengers grumbled.

"Troop trains always get priority. The Lord knows whether we'll get to Birmingham before dark at this rate," said a resigned voice behind Kay, although it was only late afternoon.

On her knee Kay held her gas mask in its case and a small holdall containing the few items she had been told to bring: washing things, pyjamas, a change of underclothes, brush and comb, slippers. It wasn't much, considering that she had no idea when she'd be returning home on leave. It had seemed odd to leave her books, clothes and belongings behind, as if she were leaving part of her identity with them.

The train crawled into a station, past allotments planted with runner beans and frilly purple-blue cabbages. A group of soldiers emerged from the station buffet and two office girls entered Kay's carriage, complaining that the train was late and there were no spare seats. A girl of about Kay's age, dressed in a smart rose-pink coat and carrying a small suitcase, hesitated on the platform before turning back to the adjoining carriage. Kay wondered whether she was going to the WAAF training depot too, and it occurred to her that this train might be carrying a number of girls to the same destination. A woman guard stepped forward to give a shrill blast on her whistle, and Kay watched the enamelled advertisements on the platform slide past and blur as the train pulled out.

She would soon be looking at flat airfields instead of the canal bridges and coal barges of the industrial and rural Midlands. Rabbits nibbled grass on the sunlit slope of a meadow, two Land Girls loaded hay on to a cart; gradually the agricultural scenery gave way to the cluttered outskirts of Birmingham, and the train slowed. Kay clutched the handle of her case and stood up, her stomach suddenly astir with butterflies.

She went through to the booking hall as instructed, and saw that quite a number of recruits, twenty or so, had arrived by the same train. They stood singly and in pairs, eyeing each other warily, clutching their cases and gas-masks. Although the weather was hot, most were dressed like Kay in jackets and tailored skirts, with one or two in flowered summer frocks. Looking at the collection of young women, all different heights and shapes and sizes, colourfully dressed and with hair carefully waved or in long film-starrish bobs, Kay found it hard to imagine them drilled into uniformity.

A WAAF and an RAF sergeant were there to meet them, the latter checking names briskly from a list, while the corporal – Kay recognised her as such by her shoulder stripes – sent those who had already been checked off to wait outside. Hearing her own name and number called, Kay answered, "Present."

The sergeant looked at her with amused exasperation. "When I call your name in future, you answer 'Yes, Sergeant,'" he told her, "loud and clear."

Embarrassed at making her first mistake so

soon, Kay followed the beckoning arm of the corporal to join the others outside. Fancy answering "present" as if she were still at school! She might look like a schoolgirl, but she didn't have to act like one.

"The transports are in the car park," the corporal said. "It's a thirty-minute drive to the camp."

WAAF drivers were standing by the tail boards of the transport lorries, and the young women climbed in to sit on benches inside, stowing their bags on the floor or on their laps. Kay found herself sitting between a tall fair girl with elegantly plucked eyebrows and a Veronica Lake hairstyle, and a horsy-looking red-head who, as soon as the lorry had moved off, announced, "Well, we may as well start getting to know one another. I'm Madge Hunter, from Canterbury," and began finding out the names and backgrounds of those around her. When she had all the names, she turned to Kay and said, "And what made you decide to join the WAAF?"

Before Kay could answer, the girl on her other side, whose name was Felicity, said promptly, "Because of the blue uniform. I wouldn't be seen dead in khaki – it does nothing for my colouring. So it was the Wrens or the WAAF, and air force blue suits me better than navy."

Some of the others giggled shyly. Madge, evidently disapproving, turned to cross-examine someone else. Felicity rolled her eyes and said to Kay in an undertone, "Who's she, our house prefect? I had enough of them at school."

Soon someone obliged Madge by asking why she had joined up. Madge replied, "My fiancé's an officer in Bomber Command. Of course I shall apply for a commission myself as soon as I can."

"The sooner the better," Felicity whispered, "as long as she doesn't end up anywhere near me."

"Shhh," Kay whispered back, stifling giggles. She had a feeling that Felicity would turn out to be fun.

The lorry turned on to a rough track, jolting over dips and ruts, and then lurched to a halt. The WAAF driver flung down the tailgate, letting in the sunlight. "Here we are."

Everyone got out and looked around with interest. They were standing in front of a camp of Nissen huts, intersected with asphalt pathways. Some were flanked by borders planted with geraniums and pansies, or vegetables. It made Kay think of the Base Hospital near Boulogne which her mother had described to her, where nurses and medical officers – and, presumably, patients – had shivered through the long damp winters of the Great War. Living conditions here must be better than that, she hoped.

The newcomers were lined up and led off to a hut, where an admin officer checked their numbers and issued them with identity discs, and then they were taken to another hut with closed curtains at the windows.

"FFI Parade next," said the corporal, and left.

"FFI? What's that?" someone asked.

"Friend or Foe Identification," Madge said knowledgeably. "It seems a strange thing to start with."

"Indeed it would be," Felicity murmured. "She's got that wrong, anyway. FFI stands for Free From Infection. It's time to strip off, girls."

Concerned glances were exchanged, and in a moment another WAAF corporal came in and confirmed what Felicity had said: they were all to strip down to their knickers and stand in line with a bath towel round their shoulders. Kay hesitated, not sure she had heard right; were they really expected to strip off, *here*, and stand almost naked in front of everyone? Felicity, quite unperturbed, started to unbutton her blouse, and others followed suit. There was no choice. Kay pushed her belongings against the wall and undressed as discreetly as she could, trying not to look at anyone else. A few moments later all the newcomers stood in line, some shivering although it wasn't cold, clutching their towels around them.

The WAAF corporal opened the door to admit a male doctor. Further anguished looks went up and down the line, especially when the officer approached the first young woman, listened to her heart with a stethoscope, checked her teeth, then pulled forward the elastic of her knickers and looked inside. It was almost as if she were a horse he was thinking of buying at an auction. The girl was then passed on to the corporal, who searched through her hair with a comb, like an ape looking for fleas. Kay steeled herself for the ordeal and looked steadfastly at the wall while the doctor carried out his perfunctory examination. Surely, she thought, they could have provided a female medical officer, and a curtained cubicle for the brief examinations? Evidently there was no sign of plague or infestation, as all the girls were passed fit and told to get dressed again.

"Just be glad you're not a man," Felicity remarked, leaving Kay to wonder what further indignities could be devised for male recruits.

The NCO, a plump young woman whose tunic buttons strained over her ample chest, was shouting at the girls to hurry, in a husky voice which suggested a capacity for barking out orders like a parade ground sergeant. Did *women* have to bawl like that, Kay wondered? "Leave your bags here. You'll come back for them after your dinners," the corporal explained.

They were led to another hut whose smell reminded Kay of school dinners. Huge mugs of tea were issued first; then cooks in white overalls doled out generous portions of sausage, mashed potato and processed peas, with steamed pudding and custard to follow. Kay took her food to a table with Felicity, a pair of Lancashire sisters and a quietly spoken West Country girl. The mess was the length of two Nissen huts; at the far end, WAAFs in uniform were eating their meal, looking at the newcomers with vague interest.

"You wouldn't think there was such a thing as rationing," one of the sisters remarked. "No wonder that NCO's so well-covered."

"Wait till they start us on square-bashing," Felicity said. "They're making sure we've got plenty of energy for that."

Kay started to eat, thinking of her mother having dried-egg-on-toast or a meagre soup in the kitchen at home, if she had bothered to make anything for herself. For the first time homesickness threatened to overcome her, and she put down her knife and fork. The atmosphere in the crowded mess was thick with the smells of custard and fried sausage, hot and oppressive.

"Eat up, love," said the younger of the Lancashire sisters. "You look as if you could do with feeding up a bit."

"Missing home?" the other said sympathetically. "Don't worry, you'll soon see your mum and dad again. Susie and me were glad to get away from ours, weren't we? Not been away from home before?"

Kay told them about school in Malvern and her visits to Ireland. She wished the sisters' motherly attentions didn't make her feel quite so childish. To divert attention from herself, she asked Felicity, "Did you really mean what you said, about choosing the WAAF for the blue uniform?"

Felicity laughed. "That was part of it. The other was to meet men, of course. On some of the bases there are forty men to one woman. My friend's on a fighter base and she says you can have a different boyfriend every night, if you want."

Susie laughed tolerantly. "Well, that's one reason for joining up. Me and Brenda were conscripted. But we'll be pleased to get a rest from housework."

They began to discuss the various WAAF trades they had in mind. The Devon girl wanted to go to a balloon base; the two sisters hoped for office work; Felicity, like Kay, wanted to be a plotter. Intrigued by Felicity, Kay found herself watching her as they ate their pudding. Felicity already seemed quite at home, undaunted by the new routines. She had an air of worldly wisdom and a quick intelligence in her blue eyes, which made her appear older than eighteen. She had found time to retouch her make-up since they had arrived, and to brush her blonde hair so that it framed her face sleekly. The clothes she wore, a grey silk blouse and lilac-coloured skirt and jacket, looked expensive and stylish. Kay did not think it would take her long to attract the boyfriends she was so keen to meet.

After the meal, the newcomers were lined up again to collect blankets and bedding, then taken to their accommodation hut. This offered little comfort: it was a Nissen hut, with a brown lino floor, rows of bare iron bedsteads, a few hard chairs, and an unlit stove in the centre with a chimney-pipe reaching up through the roof. Another corporal introduced her charges to the mysteries of 'biscuits'.

"You don't eat them – you sleep on them." She held up a square flattened cushion, like a section of mattress. "They look like dog biscuits, you see. You get three of these, and this is how you leave your bed in the morning, all tidy." She stacked three biscuits with folded blankets beside them. "We need to see through to the floor and check whether you've swept properly underneath. This is how you make your bed up at night – the sheet holds the biscuits together, like this. Think yourselves lucky," she added to someone who looked doubtful. "Aircraftmen don't get sheets. Now, choose a bed and make it up. You'll be up early – reveille is at six forty-five. The ablutions hut is next door."

Most of the newcomers opted for an early night, and within forty minutes the hut was in darkness. Kay tried to get comfortable on the unyielding biscuits, thinking regretfully of her bedroom at home with its reading lamp and bookshelves.

The next morning was spent going from one queue to another: first to have photographs taken for passes, next for typhoid inoculations, then to hand in all the civilian paraphernalia of ration books, identity cards and cloth-ing coupons. Finally came the long-awaited kitting-out, which took place in an enormous hangar-like building where NCOs presided over trestle tables of clothing. Each recruit was given a large kitbag to put everything in, and then a complete set of WAAF attire, from cap to shoes and everything in between.

"Good God, I'm not wearing those," Felicity protested, holding up a pair of knee-length blue

42

knickers. "What are they made of, old barrage balloons?"

"You'll get used to them," a corporal said cheerfully. "You can see why we call them passion-killers. The winter ones are even worse."

Kay collected together her bagful of blue-grey tunic and skirt, shirt and collar, lisle stockings, cap, underwear, belt, tie and black Oxford shoes, and went back to the adjoining hut to change. After fastening a great many buckles and buttons, she was ready to compete with nineteen other girls to look at herself in the mirror.

"You can't have your hair like that," said a disapproving corporal. "All your hair's got to be off your collar. You'd be put on a charge if you went out like that."

"Here, there's an easy way to do it," offered the West Country girl, Phyllis, who was already immaculate. "Got some kirby-grips? You get an old stocking – got a spare one? Thanks – and you roll your hair up over it like this, making a sort of sausage-shape, and pin it. Then you can keep your hair long and let it down for dances."

Within minutes Kay was looking at her un-recognisable self in the mirror, neatly buttoned and belted, topped by a blue peaked cap and shod in the heavy black Oxfords which were surprisingly comfortable. Her hair was tucked and rolled in the approved fashion, and she looked in every respect the correctly turned-out servicewoman.

It was both exciting and daunting. She was impressed by the smartness of the small figure in the glass, but for the first time she felt real qualms at giving up her civilian status. It was as if she had handed herself over to the authorities along with her ration book and identity card – which, in a way, she had. She was not an individual any more. She was 579127 ACW Leary, K., part of a unit, about to be trained to follow orders unquestioningly.

Dear Mum,

I'm a WAAF in uniform at last! You wouldn't recognise me in my best blue! If only I were a bit taller, I'd really look the part.

There are two plump sisters here who look so much like Tweedledum and Tweedledee, all squashed and buttoned into their uniforms, that I have to try not to laugh when I look at them. There are some very nice girls, but of course we'll all be split up when we get our postings, so probably I won't know any of them for very long.

We spend our time marching and drilling, doing PT, going to lectures, doing cleaning duties and having kit inspection. We spent a whole morning practising saluting, can you believe it! Longest way up, shortest way down, that's the rule. Now we have to remember to salute every officer's uniform we see. All the marching about seems a bit like playing at soldiers – we're all looking forward to starting our trades, as they call them, with more specialised training.

Kit inspection is quite a ritual! You have to put everything out on your bed, all in a certain order, and with all the clothes perfectly folded. Then you have to stand to attention while it's all checked, from your gas cape and helmet down to your "irons" – (knife, fork and spoon – we each keep our own). Woe betide you if there's something missing, even the smallest item from your sewing kit! You could be put on a charge – that seems to be the threat for all sorts of failings. It hasn't happened to anyone yet, and we're all a bit concerned, because you can be punished with something called jankers. Goodness knows what that is – no one's dared to ask!

When you write to me you must remember to put my number as well as my name. Everything in the WAAF happens by numbers. The sergeant says, "You haven't got no name any more, you've got a number!" Apparently, "if your folks don't use no number, you don't get no letters".

I'll write again soon, and meanwhile, look after yourself . . . *   *   *

Felicity flung herself on to her neatly stacked bed. "Good God! Why do they make us do all this tiresome marching about? I thought we were in the WAAF, not the Boy Scouts."

Kay sat on her own bed rubbing soaked and aching feet. "I don't mind the marching. It's the endless parading in pouring rain that strikes me as completely pointless."

"After all those injections my left arm's twice the size of my right," Felicity complained. "Anyone would think we were off to some steaming jungle in equatorial Africa, the rate they keep sticking needles into us."

"Kit inspection in half an hour," bellowed Sergeant Watkins, sticking her head round the door.

A chorus of groans greeted her disappearance, and Kay glumly contemplated her mudsplashed shoes, which would have to be restored to parade ground spotlessness within the next thirty minutes. A lot of these parades and inspections seemed to be as much a way of filling the recruits' time as fulfilling any useful purpose. Having her kit perfectly arranged wasn't going to help win the war. At least, by now, the lectures, drill and PT were alternated with IQ and aptitude tests, and interviews to select candidates for various "trades". The initial training period was drawing to a close.

"You've got a good clear voice," the trade-testing officer told Kay. "And you seem bright and quick to learn. I'm going to recommend you as a radio telephone operator."

Pleased, Kay went back to tell the others. Phyllis had asked to work on a barrage balloon crew, disappointing Kay, who had hoped that they might be posted together. Madge went about telling everyone that she was going to be chosen for Special Duties; no one else was quite sure what this meant, but it sounded most impressive.

"I shall probably have to sign the Official Secrets Act," Madge said importantly to anyone who would listen.

That night Felicity and another girl, who had gone to a YMCA dance in town, came back to camp ten minutes later than their passes allowed. They were put on a charge, which meant appearing before a senior WAAF officer, and were given as punishment a day confined to camp with extra domestic duties. Returning to the hut with Phyllis, Kay found Felicity energetically polishing the lino floor.

"Is that what I think it is?" Kay looked closely at the polisher Felicity was using. A sanitary towel was attached to the end by its two loops.

"Yes – that's how it's done in the WAAF, according to Sergeant Watkins. She'll be down on her hands and knees inspecting this when

I've finished, and you can bet it won't be good enough unless she can see every pore of her ugly face in it. I don't think she's taken much of a liking to me," Felicity said cheerfully.

"You don't seem exactly fond of her."

"I wouldn't have minded if the dance had been worth it. It was full of WAAFs and ATS girls, hardly a man in sight. Not my idea of a night out."

"Why were you late, then, if it was so dull?"

"We went to the Duke of Wellington pub." Felicity splashed liquid polish over the floor. "Out of my way, girls. Us janker-wallahs mustn't be distracted."

Jankers explained at last, Kay thought, or rather demonstrated. For some reason the word had always made her think of medieval torture, instead of which it was more like a schoolgirl punishment. At times, giggling in the hut with the others when the corporal wasn't around, she felt that the whole experience was like being at school; there was the same healthy disrespect for minor authority figures, the same triumph when a trivial rule infringement was overlooked. There was fun along with the discipline, but Kay was eager to progress to the next stage; at present she was in limbo between her former self and the accomplished WAAF she aimed to be, carrying out her duties indispensably.

On the final day, before a special passing-out parade, everyone gathered in the assembly hall for details of postings or further training. This time tomorrow, Kay thought, we'll all be going off separately, and have to start making friends all over again . . .

". . . Aircraftwoman Hunter, M. – Special Duties . . ."

Madge had got what she wanted, then, definitely a cut above the humbler roles of cook, clerk or driver. She'd be sent to a secret destination of which she'd be informed later, the admin officer said.

". . . Aircraftwoman Larkins, W. – M.T. Driver, Bardney . . ."

Kay waited impatiently as the admin officer reached the bottom of a page and turned over slowly. Any moment now, she would know. Her immediate future would be fixed, decided; there would be no arguing with the decision. The faces around her were excited, baffled or disappointed, according to individual hopes and expectations.

"579127 Aircraftwoman Leary, K. – Radio Telephone Operator, Windersby . . ."

"You lucky thing," Felicity whispered. "Wait and see what ghastly dump they land me in."

"Pearson . . . Peters . . . Rivenall . . ." The admin officer sounded as bored as if she were reading a telephone directory.

"I wish I didn't come right at the bottom of the alphabet," Felicity muttered. "I always have to wait till last."

"Shh—"

"Aircraftwoman Whiting, F. – Radio Telephone Operator, Windersby . . ."

"We're posted together!"

Kay and Felicity exchanged surprised grins. What a piece of luck, Kay thought; she had no idea where or what Windersby was or how they were expected to get there, but having Felicity for company would be a definite bonus.

WINDERSBY

"*I*t's Bomber Command," Kay said on the station platform, looking at the typed instructions she and Felicity had been given. "Not fighters."

"Yes, I know. I can't believe our luck, though." Felicity leaned back against the wooden seat. "We could have ended up on one of those all-girl balloon stations, like Phyllis, or doing dreary office work miles from the nearest airfield. What's the matter? Wasn't that what you wanted, to be on an operational station?"

"Yes, but . . ." Kay hesitated, and then admitted, "My mother won't like it."

Felicity grinned. "My parents didn't want me to be in the WAAF at all. They seem to think there's something immoral about it."

"Do they? I thought my mother was the only person who felt like that."

"Oh no. Aircrew, for the use of, that's how they think WAAFs are seen. *Only suitable for a certain kind of girl,*" Felicity mimicked. "Is that what your mum says?"

"No," Kay said, surprised. "Do people really think that?"

"Oh yes," Felicity said airily. "Officers' groundsheets – haven't you heard that one?"

Kay stared at her and then felt herself blushing as she realised what the phrase meant.

"Kay, you're such an innocent," Felicity said, laughing. "Where have you been?"

Kay felt that this was unfair. She may be innocent in some ways, but she was certainly not the only one. She remembered the last of the Health Lectures they had been given, which had been all about venereal disease, with slides of horrible ulcers and disfigurements. For some reason the lecture had taken place immediately before lunch, and Kay had not been the only one unable to face her meal. But at least she had some idea how these diseases were transmitted, which the lecture hadn't actually made clear; one or two of the girls had seemed little the wiser. But officers' groundsheets! Did some girls really behave like that?

"Surely people don't think that about *all* the WAAFs – what you said," she objected. "I know it was hard for them to be taken seriously at the beginning of the war, without proper

52

uniforms or anything, but I thought everyone had accepted it now. WAAFs do all sorts of important jobs."

"Yes, I expect you're right. Everyone except my parents, that is." Felicity looked at her watch. "The train's late. Anyway, what is it your mum won't like, then?"

"Me being on a bomber station. Fighters would have been all right, but she hates the bombing raids on Germany."

Felicity's eyebrows shot up. "Why? What does she think we ought to do? Sit here and wave a white flag at the Luftwaffe?"

Kay tried to explain: "She thinks defence is one thing, but aggression another. She says, how can we criticise the Nazis, if we're killing German civilians?"

"But that's ridiculous!" Felicity exclaimed. "At least we're giving as good as we get."

Kay had expected no other response. Having rashly repeated her mother's views at school, she knew that they were untypical and unpopular. Luckily, Alice chose not to broadcast her opinions, but simply got on quietly with her work in helping the victims of war. Otherwise, with her membership of the Peace Pledge Union and her visits to Germany between the wars, she would risk denunciation as a German sympathiser. Kay had quickly learned that it was unwise to draw attention to her mother's stance, and she certainly had no intention of doing so on an air force base.

"Anyway, I can't see what difference it makes where you're posted," Felicity said. "It's all the RAF, isn't it? We're going to be doing something useful, and we're going to be on a big station with lots going on. There are bound to be dances and concerts, and we can go to Lincoln on our day off. Your mum'll soon get used to it. I should think yourself lucky."

They arrived in Lincolnshire in the midst of a heavy summer shower. Driving rain obscured the landscape, and the windscreen wipers of the RAF van which met them at the station could barely cope with the downpour. Kay stared out of the streaming windows to see what she could of their surroundings, but could distinguish only hedges and the blurred shapes of buildings.

"Straight off the North Sea, this is." The sergeant driver had to shout to be heard above the drumming of rain on the roof. "Nothing between us and the coast except potato fields and sheep. What are you two, then? Clerks?"

"We're going to be R/T operators," Kay said proudly.

"Oh yes?" The driver slowed, and jerked a thumb towards the side of the road. "If it wasn't so blooming wet, you'd see the aircraft over the hedge here. Lancasters. We're on the edge of the airfield now."

Kay felt her stomach lurch with nervousness and excitement as she peered through the blur to see if she could make out the shapes of the heavy bombers.

The driver left his passengers and their kitbags outside the Guard Room, where they scurried quickly out of the rain to check in. Close by was a large square building, its brick-work almost entirely obscured by ivy – the "Waafery", the driver had said. Here the newcomers were given a late supper. They ate hungrily after the long and frustrating rail journey, during which they hadn't been able to get so much as a cup of tea. Afterwards, an admin officer took them to collect bedding from the store and then showed them to their accommodation, a brick hut close to the Waafery. Kay looked around with interest. It was identical to the Nissen hut at the depot but with more personal touches: photographs pinned above beds, and books and letters lying about on the wooden table and on lockers. Kay and Felicity would no longer be sharing with new recruits but with WAAFs of various trades who knew their jobs and were familiar with station routines. Some beds were neatly stacked, while others were made up ready for their owners to return. A plump girl with her shirt hanging outside her skirt sat with her feet on the tortoise stove writing a letter, while three others sat at a table playing cards and another slept flat out on her bed, fully dressed.

The girl at the stove stood up and stretched. "You must be the new sprogs."

"The new what?"

"Sprogs. New recruits. Sorry – you'll get used to RAF slang before long. There are your beds, down at that end. Ghastly night, isn't it? At least there are no ops tonight to keep you awake. The crews have been stood down because of the weather."

She showed them the way to the ablutions block, which meant crossing an expanse of soaking grass. They got ready for bed, and lay talking in hushed voices until Felicity dozed off. Kay lay awake for a long time afterwards. She wished she wasn't such a raw recruit, with no specialised knowledge whatsoever. She stirred uncomfortably on her biscuits and listened to the rain battering the blacked-out windows. Now that Felicity was asleep, Kay's doubts overcame her excitement, and she wished she had gone off like some of the other recruits for three or four weeks' further training instead of being posted straight to an airfield. There must be hundreds of people on this base, all knowing exactly what was required of them. They would all be brisk and efficient, with no patience for a novice's mistakes. If only I could be like Felicity, Kay thought; she doesn't seem worried at all . . . if only I didn't feel such an impostor.

It didn't seem quite as daunting in the morning. The day was cool and fine, with a clear sky of freshly washed blue. Breakfast in the Waafery dining-room was a time-consuming nuisance. Before they could start work, Kay and Felicity had to get various forms signed at the Orderly Room, the Pay Section and various other parts of the camp. The base was divided by a road separating the domestic sites from the technical buildings and the airfield itself, whose smooth expanse stretched away farther than the eye could see. By its perimeter were enormous hangars, camouflaged in brown and green. Several Lancasters stood in front of the hangars – giant four-engined bombers with snub noses and enormous wing spans, which made Kay think of predatory monsters. Aircrew were walking about from one place to another, some of them just boys, not much older than Kay. She felt awed by the terrible responsibilities and dangers they faced. It put her own sense of inadequacy into perspective.

When they had collected all the signatures they needed, she and Felicity reported back to the Guard Room and were told that they could now go to the Flying Control Office to begin their duties. This was an ugly square building facing the airfield, with a brick tower surmounted by a viewing platform with a hand-rail.

"That must be where people stand to watch the bombers coming back," Felicity said. "Like in the films."

Kay hesitated outside the sandbagged entrance, and it was Felicity who led the way in and up a flight of stairs. She knocked on an interior door and entered the room inside, followed by Kay. It was a long, narrow room facing directly on to the airfield; a bench ran along the whole length of the window on that side. It was occupied by several airmen and two WAAFs, and a grey-haired officer in horn-rimmed glasses, whose uniform carried the wings of the Royal Flying Corps, showing that he was a veteran of the last war. His tunic sleeves were decorated with three bands, a narrow one between two wide ones, denoting Squadron Leader. The two girls remembered to salute, and explained who they were.

It was immediately clear that they hadn't been expected at all; indeed the squadron leader seemed rather put out by their arrival.

"We've got two other WAAFs under training already." He indicated the two sitting by radio sets at the bench. "Now I suppose we'll have to reorganise the shifts again." He consulted his watch. "You'd better go and get your lunch. By the time you come back we'll have things sorted out. One of you can start on the next shift."

Rebuffed, the pair walked back to the Waaf-ery dining-room, to be turned away again: it was full of women who had come off an early shift. "You can get your meal at the cook-house," a corporal told them. "WAAF can eat over there, now there's so many of us."

Warm greasy smells and a haze of cigarette smoke filled the air in the main cookhouse. The tables were crowded with WAAFs, groundcrew and aircrew in a variety of attire: best blue, battledress, three or four sergeant pilots in flying boots and leather jackets. Felicity brightened, attracting several male glances. She and Kay collected their sausage and chips and sat down at one of the few empty tables, where they were soon joined by a man of about thirty with sandy hair and a moustache.

"You mustn't mind old Bothers," he said, and Kay realised that he was one of the staff from the Flying Control Office. "Squadron Leader Bothwell, I mean, the FCO. He's not all that keen on having girls up there, though it's high time he was used to it. Mike Anderson," he introduced himself, holding out a broad freckled hand to each of them in turn. "No relation to the shelters."

Kay and Felicity told him their names, and he

continued, "Can either of you sing? Dance? Play the piano?"

"Goodness, and I thought it was just a matter of giving landing instructions," Felicity said. "We're expected to entertain the crews over the air waves too, are we?"

Mike grinned. "I mean for concerts and pantomimes, Miss Clever. Me and Charlie Fox like to get things organised now and then, to cheer everyone up. We're always on the look-out for likely talent."

"I wouldn't mind. I can dance a bit," Felicity said. "What about you, Kay? It'd be fun, wouldn't it?"

Kay agreed that it might be, though she was not sure whether she wanted to commit herself quite so early to making a public spectacle of herself. After drinking their tea they returned to the Control Office. Felicity was told to come back again at half-past four, while Kay was to start immediately, with Mike as her tutor. The flying control officer went off for his own lunch, and the atmosphere in the office lightened immediately. Kay's alarm at being expected to learn on the job, with no preliminary training, was assuaged by the kindly presence of Mike, who began on a brisk and competent run through the basic procedures. She sat at the bench looking out at the wide expanse of the airfield and the level horizon. A few heavy planes were moving slowly up to the runway, and engines droned overhead as another came in to land, given instructions by the WAAF at the next transmitter.

"It's just training flights at the moment," Mike said. "Bumps and circuits, with sprog pilots. These twin-engined jobs are Wellingtons – Wimpeys, we call them. It'll be all Lancasters on ops. You can put the earphones on in a minute when I've shown you what to do. You've got two microphones, see – that one for long range and this one for local frequency. We're on local now, but you use long range on ops to pick up the first plane over the coast on its way back. Then you change to local as soon as they're in range, for landing instructions. You push this button to transmit – don't take any notice of the crackle on the loudspeaker. We use the loudspeakers for night ops. When a pilot calls down wanting to land, you answer like this: 'Hello F-Fox,' (or whatever he's called), 'this is Blackrock answering,' (that's us), 'receiving you loud and clear, strength niner, over.' You work in pairs, one of you transmitting, the other logging all conversations in this book. You've got to write down everything that's said over R/T. It gets easier when you learn procedure, and the abbreviations. Strength niner refers to the signal strength – two is very faint, niner loud and clear, only you

61

say niner on R/T because nine might sound like five. For five you say fife."

Before long Kay had the earphones on and was being prompted by Mike to give landing instructions to a nervous-sounding pilot circling somewhere overhead. When the plane came into view, and performed a wobbly landing in front of the Control Office, she felt almost as proud as if she had done it herself. It all seemed rather congenial – cups of tea and friendly chatter at the Control Bench between take-offs and landings, good-natured criticism of the sprog pilots' efforts, the grounded planes moving about like browsing dinosaurs, and the level countryside spreading out in the sunlight towards a hazy horizon. It was very different from the scenes of silent tension in plotting-rooms which Kay had imagined. It was a pleasant introduction to her duties, but far from the real thing, when planes were returning from night raids, or ops as she was learning to call them. She thought of planes coming in thick and fast, some damaged, perhaps; herself panicking, with no friendly Mike by her side to tell her what to do.

He told her that she would spend two afternoons each week having specialised training at the transmitting station, working towards an exam. "When you've passed that, you'll be a qualified R/T operator." He patted his tunic sleeve. "Then you'll get a 'sparks' badge, like this."

"Do I start on the shifts straight away?"

"That's right. When you're on shifts you do a four-hour watch and an eight-hour," Mike explained. "It sounds a lot to do in a day, but you do get a day off in between. And you always get a full day off after night duty."

There were various maps and charts on the walls behind them, which Kay resolved to study. Wooden models of aircraft – British and German – hung from the ceiling, each one clearly labelled. Behind the bench was a heavy black-out curtain, pulled back at present, but which Mike told her would be closed at night to separate the Control bench from the main part of the office. He showed her a big chalkboard on one wall, ruled into columns which were left blank at present; this was used for checking each plane out and then in again when they went on operations.

Kay left the Control Office at the end of her session feeling immeasurably wiser than when she went in, although she guessed that Felicity, going in for the evening shift, might have a more eventful time. Lying in bed that night, Kay heard the roar of heavy planes taking off, one after another. She thought about the crews and wondered what it would be like to take off in a plane loaded with bombs, to fly across the hostile enemy coast dodging the flak and the fighters, and to do that not just once but time and time again . . . She fell asleep rehearsing the radio alphabet: A-Apple, B-Baker, C-Charlie, until the letters circled in her mind like aircraft waiting to land.

Next morning, Felicity was matter-of-fact about the previous night's raid, as nonchalant as if she had been doing the job for months. "It was just a routine trip, apparently. Gardening, they call it – laying mines along the enemy coast."

"And did they all come back?"

"I imagine so. I wouldn't know – I came off duty before any of them were due. Did you see the notice on the Waafery board?" Felicity said, with far more interest. "There's a dance tomorrow night in the Sergeants' Mess. It's lucky we'll both be off-duty. You will come, won't you?"

Kay agreed. After their first afternoon at the transmitting station, learning about daily inspections for the equipment they were using, they had a quick meal at the cookhouse and then hurried back to their hut to get ready. They pressed their uniforms and polished the buttons, put on clean shirts and added dabs of perfume for what little glamour could be mustered at a uniformed dance. Encouraged by Felicity, Kay put on more make-up than she usually wore and looked doubtfully at the result in the mirror. She wasn't sure that it didn't make her look younger rather than older. She wished she had Felicity's poise.

"Someone told me you can get away with silk stockings at a dance," Felicity said, looking down ruefully at her lisle-clad legs. "I shall get some when we go into town. These make me feel about as glamorous as a Victorian schoolmarm."

In the Sergeants' Mess, the dining-hall had been cleared to make room for dancing. There was a bar at one end, at which airmen stood two or three deep; at the other end was an improvised band – piano, saxophone and drums – playing popular dance tunes. Skeins of cigarette smoke hung in the air above the few couples who whirled and swayed to the music, although it seemed that the evening hadn't properly begun yet and most people were standing in groups chatting. An airman immediately came up and asked Felicity to dance, leading her away. Left on her own, Kay felt awkward and out of place, not sure what to do. The gathering was predominantly male, not at all like the decorous and closely chaperoned school dances she had attended in the past. She would have liked something to drink, but did not want to push through the wall of men to the bar. For a cowardly moment she considered sneaking out and going back to the hut; in the whole crowded room there was not one person she knew, apart from Felicity, who was talking animatedly to her partner. Deciding that she would feel less conspicuous if she sat on one of the chairs lining the walls, she started to make her way between the chattering groups.

"You look about as out of place as I feel," said a male voice behind her. "Have you just arrived?"

The speaker was a dark-haired young man of perhaps twenty. His uniform pocket carried the brevet denoting aircrew, with a single wing and the letter N, for navigator. He was holding a glass and appeared to be on his own.

"At Windersby, you mean, or at the dance?" Kay said. "Yes to both, anyway. I've been here two days."

"I'm new as well," the young man said. His voice had a slight Welsh lilt. "Your first posting?" When Kay nodded he said, "Mine, too. Could I get you a drink?"

Kay asked for the first thing she could think of, which was port (probably an odd choice for a dance, she realised immediately she had asked for it; wasn't port supposed to be passed round the table after dinner, with cigars?). But her new acquaintance nodded, and went off to get it. When he returned, they sat down together; he asked what her name was and told her that his was David Evans.

"Have you flown on ops yet?" Kay sipped the port, which she didn't really like, and made a mental note to consult Felicity about suitable drinks.

He shook his head. "That's a pleasure yet to come. The rest of my crew are old hands – nearly at the end of their tour. They've all been together since they formed up. They fly A-Able, in B Flight. I've been brought in to replace a navigator who was killed. What do you do?"

Kay told him that she was a trainee R/T operator and might be guiding his plane in when it came back from ops.

"I'll make sure the pilot asks for you by name, then," David said.

They chatted for a while about their training. David had wanted to be a pilot, but had been selected as a navigator instead at grading school. He came from Monmouth, where Kay and her mother had stayed once on a holiday; soon they were deep in conversation about favourite walks in the wooded valleys of the River Wye and in the Black Mountains. David was quietly spoken and attentive, very different from the brash types Felicity seemed to favour; his lively dark eyes were fixed intently on Kay's face as she spoke. She decided that she liked him.

After a while he asked her to dance. Felicity swayed by in the arms of a new partner and smiled approvingly as they took to the now crowded dance floor. Neither Kay nor David was a particularly accomplished dancer, but David held her carefully, steering a path through the jostling couples. They danced together for the next four pieces, and then a curly-haired sergeant with pilot's wings on his brevet clapped a hand on David's shoulder.

"Hang on a minute there, Evans boyo. Sprogs can't expect to keep all the pretty girls to themselves. Dance this one with me, sweetheart."

He grabbed hold of Kay without waiting for her to accept, and swung her away with far more expertise than David had shown, talking glibly all the time and paying her extravagant compliments.

Kay would have preferred to carry on dancing with David. Wishing she had had enough presence of mind to refuse, she excused herself as soon as the music finished, intending to find him again. But she could not see him at the side of the hall where they had been sitting. He must have joined the rest of his crew, or found another partner.

DARKY

Mike yawned loudly. "Nearly time to turn in. And a whole day off tomorrow."

It had been an uneventful watch. On the late afternoon to midnight shift, even when there were ops, there was not much to do after recording the aircraft code letters and departure times. Unless it had been a very early take-off, different staff would be on duty by the time the planes came back. The list of aircraft on the Battle Order for tonight was headed by A-Able, and Kay wondered whether the navigator she had met at the dance would be on board. As she did not know the name of his pilot, the only crew member listed on the board, there was no way of knowing.

When things were quiet, the duty staff passed the time by reading, sewing or writing letters.

These pastimes were officially forbidden, so books, writing pads and sewing kits had to be quickly concealed in respirator cases if a senior officer entered the room. Kay glanced up from the letter she was surreptitiously writing to her mother. The clock showed a quarter to midnight. Outside, the airfield was in complete darkness. A pale moon, appearing from time to time behind wreaths of cloud, was not strong enough to throw the landscape into relief.

"Are you going home tomorrow?" she asked Mike, whose wife lived in Peterborough with their two children.

Before Mike could answer, the radio trans-mitter crackled into life.

"Hello, Darky. Hello, Darky."

Kay knew that this was an emergency call from an aircraft lost or otherwise in trouble.

"Quick," Mike said. Everyone in the room was suddenly alert. The other WAAF on duty went through to the wireless operators' room to fetch the duty officer, who had gone there for a chat.

Kay had been trained in Darky procedure and knew what to do. She pressed the button to transmit and gave the standard response. "Hello, Nemo. This is Windersby. Receiving strength four. Hello, Nemo."

"Windersby," the voice came again, indistinctly. "This is Lighthouse D-Dog. Request urgent permission to land."

Squadron Leader Bothwell appeared beside Kay and she glanced up at him for confirmation. "Hello, Lighthouse D-Dog, this is Windersby. Prepare to land. Lighthouse D-Dog, prepare to land."

The runway lighting had been turned on, and someone was at the telephone alerting the emergency services.

"Call him again," Mike said.

"Hello, Lighthouse D-Dog. Clear to land. Emergency services standing by. Are you in trouble?"

Of course he's in trouble, she thought, use your sense, otherwise he wouldn't be using the Darky call . . .

The pilot's voice came back, a little more distinctly, the voice of a nervous boy: "Extensive damage to tail section . . . rear gunner badly injured . . . one engine u/s . . ."

The drone of the engine could be heard overhead now, and one of the wireless operators ran up to the balcony to see.

"Sounds like a Lanc," he shouted back, while Mike identified the call sign as belonging to a base in Suffolk.

"Windersby, I'm coming in," came the thin frightened sound of the pilot's voice. "Trying to land . . . I can't get . . ." His voice trailed off, and Kay imagined him wrestling with the controls of the stricken Lancaster, his entire concentration needed to nurse it down, to save himself and his crew. He must be a thousand feet away at most, so close, yet none of the Control Room staff could do more than sit tautly at attention, waiting. No one could do anything except the pilot himself, faced with his terrifying responsibility.

And then the plane shot into view, much too fast, plummeted awkwardly to touch down and then careered out of control across the runway.

"He won't stop in time . . ." the other WAAF exclaimed.

With a sickening crash and rending of metal and concrete, the wounded Lancaster plunged into an outbuilding by the perimeter fence. At once, too quickly to see where it started, there was a gush of fire as the entire plane was engulfed. Black smoke poured from the burning fuel, drifting along the ground like an obliterating fog. Fragments of metal were hurled from the machine by the force of the explosion of heat. The flames leaped and brightened as they consumed the fuselage, turning the dying plane into a brilliant torch against the darkness.

There was a shocked silence in the Control Room. The crash wagon was scurrying across the airfield, but it was clear that no one could have survived. Kay knew that she was looking at the funeral pyre of seven men.

Squadron Leader Bothwell went out to check for himself. Kay looked at the radio transmitter, a failed lifeline. She felt sick, numbed by the realisation that the pilot she had been speaking to just a few moments earlier was certainly dead.

The clock showed seven minutes to midnight. The incident had taken hardly any time at all. Minutes previously those seven airmen had been living, breathing individuals. Now they were probably unidentifiable remains. Their names would be rubbed off a blackboard somewhere, and they would become statistics to be added to the tally of losses.

Some of the Control staff started to discuss the incident, speculating on what previous damage the plane must have suffered and whether the pilot could have reduced his landing speed. Kay was too stunned to say anything at all. Mike, shaking his head sadly, completed the details in the log. When the next shift arrived at midnight, Kay scuttled down the stairs and leaned against the wall outside. Firemen were pumping extinguishing foam over the flames, against which the figures of the redundant ambulance crew were silhouetted; the tattered skeleton of one wing tip pointed skywards.

Acrid smells of burning oil and fuselage drifted across the field. The wreckage would have to be cleared up quickly so that the airfield was ready for its own returning Lancasters. Kay remembered the frightened voice of the pilot during his last fateful moments; she must have been the last person he had spoken to. A choking sob rose in her throat and she turned away, her eyes blurring.

"Kay. Kay." Firm hands took hold of her shoulders and she blinked furiously, recognising Mike's voice. He said, "It was awful, I know, but it must have been quick. They couldn't have known much about it, poor beggars."

"We don't know that." His soothing tone made her tears flow all the more. She groped in her tunic pocket for a handkerchief. "The pilot must have struggled home all the way across the sea and then thought he . . . thought he was safe when he saw our runway . . . and the rear gunner was already injured . . ."

"You mustn't let yourself dwell on it," Mike said, "thinking about what it must have been like. Here, have this one." He handed her his own folded handkerchief. The flickering light from the dying flames illuminated his features. "It's hard for you, your first time. Seeing it happen right in front of you like that. A bit different from just looking at a blank space on a board. But you'll get used to it. You have to. We all have to."

"I know." Kay blew her nose. Planes failed to return from ops, she knew that. She would have to get used to filling in her log and going off duty and treating it as a normal night's work. There would always be new crews to fill the gaps; the factories were churning out new Lancasters to replace the burnt fragments being cleared up from runways. This was a war, and people got killed in wars. She could hardly pretend that she hadn't known that.

"Come on," Mike said. "I'll walk you back to the Waafery and you can tidy yourself up and have a good hot cup of tea."

Tea, the universal panacea. Kay let Mike take her arm and lead her purposefully across the dark maze of the camp, following the bobbing oval of light from his torch. She was grateful for his kindness, and that it hadn't been Squadron Leader Bothwell who had found her crying. He hadn't welcomed girls in the office, Mike had said. The last thing he'd want would be droopy females weeping all over the place. It would doubtless be taken as a sign of feminine weakness, to get yourself all worked up about a commonplace little thing like death. At least Mike didn't seem to mind, or to think less of her. He seemed to understand.

* * *

"You just worked, and tried to forget about it that way," Alice had said once, when Kay asked how she had coped with the daily tragedies of a Great War hospital. "Work was the best anaesthetic, and there was always plenty of it."

Kay's working hours, accommodation and food were far better than her mother could have dreamed of, squelching round a tented hospital in the depths of winter, but the routines of camp life did have similar effect. It was difficult to get used to the changing patterns of sleep and work required by the shift system; after two weeks, Kay and Felicity were moved into a small room in the pre-war married quarters, where they could sleep undisturbed after coming off a late or overnight watch. Their new accommodation offered more comfort than the sparse brick hut; there was a small kitchen with a stove, ironing board and supply of coal, and a bathroom – no more tramping over wet grass to the ablutions block. Kay and Felicity were usually on different shifts and met only between times or on their training afternoons; Kay usually worked alongside Stephanie, the other R/T operator. Felicity had already acquired a boyfriend, a sergeant pilot she had met at the dance, and had been out several times to the Hare and Hounds pub in the village with him and his friends, or with him alone.

"You ought to get yourself a boyfriend,"

Felicity told Kay. "What about that nice-looking navigator you were dancing with the other night?"

"I haven't seen him since then."

"You don't try hard enough."

No one could accuse Felicity of not trying hard enough. Kay watched her getting ready to go out, holding up a hand-mirror and emphasising the arch of her eyebrows with dark pencil.

"You ought to come out with us one night," Felicity offered. "Bill wouldn't mind."

"Perhaps," Kay said cautiously, thinking of the raucous group she sometimes saw in the cookhouse.

But a few days later Felicity dropped Bill in favour of a good-looking Canadian flight engineer. Kay felt in any case that she would prefer to make her own arrangements; she was not sure that she could keep up with Felicity, or that she wanted to. Her hours away from the Control Office were occupied with training at the transmitter station, PT sessions twice a week and once or twice a game of netball, and Domestic Evening every Wednesday; sometimes there was a concert, film or gramophone recital. Kay became friendly with Stephanie, a small auburn-haired girl with a cat-like face, who went about her work quietly and efficiently.

Kay liked the friendly atmosphere in the

Watch Office. Squadron Leader Bothwell had thawed slightly, and the others had immediately accepted her as part of the team. Mike and the other corporal, Simon, a man of about thirty, had more than once invited Kay and Stephanie out to the Hare and Hounds on an off-duty evening, with two of the W A A Fs from the Meteorology Office. There Kay met Charlie Fox, a ground engineer – "just an erk," he described himself – who seemed to be everyone's friend. He was stockily built, about twenty-three or four, with fox-red hair to suit his name; his gift for mimicry and fund of anecdotes made him universally popular. He was organising a revue concert, and tried to sign Kay up for the cast.

"Can you sing? Joyce and Stephanie need a third girl to do *Three Little Maids from School*, from *The Mikado*. We had three to start with, but the third one got posted away. How would you fancy stepping in?"

"But I've never sung in public before," Kay protested.

"Oh, go on. It's just a bit of fun."

Finally she agreed to go to one of the rehearsals, expecting to hear no more about it afterwards; she didn't think much of her singing voice. But when she did attend Charlie was enthusiastic, full of ideas for Japanese costumes and wigs.

It was a bonus to be within reach of Lincoln

for days off. On a hot day in late September, Kay and Felicity caught an early bus into the city and spent the morning exploring the cathedral and the surrounding medieval streets which spilled steeply down the hillside towards the river. Lincoln seemed to have given itself over to entertaining off-duty air force personnel from the many bases which surrounded it; uniforms out-numbered civilian dress in the streets and cafés. A newspaper seller's chalkboard read "RUSSIANS RECAPTURE SMOLENSK". People have fought and died, Kay thought, for a place called Smolensk that I've never even heard of. At Windersby it's easy to forget that it isn't just the RAF's war. The Poles, the Jews, the Russians – thousands, millions of people are involved, across countries, across continents . . . on too big a scale to take in.

"Four whole years of war," she said, "four years this month. It seems like half my life, does it to you? But there are some good signs, aren't there – the Allies in Italy, and the Russian advances? Do you think it can go on much longer?"

Felicity shrugged. "What did your mother say," she asked, "about you being in Bomber Command? You haven't said any more about it."

"She didn't say anything at all in her letters," Kay said. "I mean, apart from asking about the work, and hoping we get enough food and sleep and that sort of thing. I'd almost have preferred her to be angry about it. It seems so unlike her to say nothing."

"There you are," Felicity said. "I said you were making a problem where there wasn't one. She obviously didn't mind as much as you expected."

"My cousin's flying bombers as well now," Kay said. "He's called in to see her."

A card had come from Stephen a few days ago, a picture postcard showing King's College Chapel at Cambridge. *So we've both ended up in Bomber Command after all*, Stephen had written. *I dropped in at Aunt Alice's when I was in London last week – really an excuse to show off my pilot's wings. I'm at a place called Wratting Common – a long way from you, but perhaps I can get myself diverted to Windersby some time* . . .

All Alice had written about the visit was *Stephen looked very well*. Kay hoped she hadn't been aloof with him.

"She's obviously got used to the idea, with two of you in the family," Felicity said. "She's probably proud of you both."

Kay wasn't so sure, but did not pursue the subject. After lunch in a cheap and cheerful restaurant, Felicity suggested hiring a rowing boat at Brayford Pool. It was a hot, lazy afternoon with little to suggest the coming of autumn. The sun dazzled, glinting off the water, and the heat struck through the fabric of Kay's uniform as she scrambled into the rowing boat.

"You can row first," Felicity told Kay. "I fancy lying here like Cleopatra in her barge."

The boatman handed over the oars and untied the painter, and the little boat bobbed away into the river basin.

"Go that way." Felicity pointed at the river's narrow downstream course between buildings. "You get the best views from there, further along."

Felicity knew Lincoln well, having visited it several times before from her home in Leicester. She had never spoken much about her home or family, and Kay asked her about them now, to the accompaniment of the steady plash of oars. They passed beneath a medieval house which was built right over the river, like a bridge. Felicity lay back, trailing a hand in the water and gazing at the ripples it made.

"We're just an ordinary family," she said. "Mother, father, elder brother, me."

"Is your brother in the forces?" Kay wondered why Felicity hadn't mentioned him before.

"Oh, yes," Felicity said, as if the subject bored her. "He's in the Navy. A Fleet Air Arm officer, based in Orkney at the moment. He was in the Navy before war broke out. A regular Navy type – pink gins in the mess and all that."

"And your parents?"

"Daddy's a local magistrate." Felicity yawned and stretched her arms above her head. "And my mother's a WVS organiser. She's got all sorts of people billeted at our house at the moment."

"It's a big house, then?"

"Yes – well, pretty big. Enough to take quite a few servants to run it, before the war. Not so many now, of course."

Felicity's background was obviously very different from Kay's. But Kay was surprised by the bored indifference with which she spoke of her family. She had made no mention of going home on leave, even though she could surely have got there and back in a day. Nor, Kay reflected, did she seem to spend much time writing to her parents. Felicity had the complete family which Kay herself had often wished for, but she did not seem very happy with it.

They had emerged from the crowded buildings of the town and could look straight up to the cathedral, high on its mound. Its three limestone towers were golden in the afternoon sunlight.

"I suppose they'd like you to get a commission, like your brother?" Kay said.

Felicity pulled a face. "What they'd like, and what I choose to do, are usually very different things. You're the one who should be thinking of being an officer. You're the clever one, with your Higher Certificate. I cleared out of school as soon as I could." She looked at Kay with a slow teasing smile. "You could be one of those pi-jawed duty officers who comes round to check that there's no fluff under the beds and that everyone's doing their sewing on Domestic Night like good little girls. I could just see you, all prim and disapproving . . ."

Kay half stood, laughing, and raised an oar so that cold drops of water showered down Felicity's neck.

"Ow, get off!" Felicity squealed. "I was only joking – Mind out – we're going to hit the bank . . .

Kay looked round, saw that they were on collision course with a moored houseboat, brandished the oars and almost lost her balance. The rowing boat swayed perilously. After a struggle, she got both oars working in unison instead of in opposition and resumed her steady course downriver.

"I'm going to bail out," Felicity said, fanning herself, "if that's the best you can do. I'd hate to see you in a Lancaster at fourteen thousand feet."

"There'd be no problem at all," Kay retorted, "if I had a half decent navigator . . .'

OPS

Ops tonight. Aircrew were straggling towards the Briefing Room. The windows were closed and shuttered, and a WAAF intelligence officer was checking the crews in. Kay was on her way to the cookhouse for tea, after which she would try to get some sleep before her night watch. It would be a big raid tonight, to judge by the numbers funnelling in at the door. Among them she recognised the sergeant who had interrupted her dance with the young navigator. He saw her too, and gave her a cheerful wave. He did not look at all concerned, as if flying on ops were no more exciting than going to a sergeants' mess dance, but some of the younger aircrew looked less at ease, laughing a little too loudly at each other's jokes to hide their nervousness. Some of them were probably going on their first night raid.

By now Kay had experienced night ops during her midnight-to-eight shifts, but her impression that this was to be more than a routine mine-laying trip or minor operation was confirmed when she went on duty at midnight. Twenty-four aircraft were listed on the Battle Order board as having taken off. The first was A-Able, with the name of its pilot, S/P Clifford. That must be the curly-haired sergeant pilot. She wondered whether Stephen's name, Pilot Officer Smallwood, was chalked up on the board at Wratting Common tonight.

Squadron Leader Bothwell said that over five hundred aircraft from various stations were on the raid: Lancasters, Halifaxes, Stirlings and the lighter, higher-flying Mosquitoes. The target was Kassel, east of the Ruhr Valley industrial area, which had received such heavy bombing earlier in the year.

"There's a big aircraft factory there – Henschels," Simon told Kay. "That'll be the main target." Mike was not on duty tonight.

Kay was familiar by now with some of the recent innovations to improve the accuracy of bombing. Pathfinder squadrons would go ahead to indicate the targets with coloured markers; more sophisticated bombs packed with pyrotechnic candles had replaced the earlier "Pink Pansies", which the Germans had learned to imitate and use as decoys. Over the enemy coast, the bomb aimers dropped "Window" out of a special chute – strips of aluminium-coated paper which confused the German radar sets with false echoes. There were also various target-finding devices: "Gee" and "Oboe", which were used to co-ordinate pulses sent out from coastal stations, and H2S, which was less reliable but had a limitless range, and was carried by the planes of the Pathfinder squadrons. Tonight, there was to be a diversionary raid which would drop large quantities of Window and coloured indicators elsewhere, to draw the German fighters away from the main target.

"They got E-Easy off all right, then," Simon said, looking at the board. "Charlie Fox thought she might not be able to go when I saw him this morning. Said she had trouble with her starboard generator before her air test."

It was a standing joke that Charlie Fox considered himself as ground engineer to be the rightful owner of E-Easy; he handed her over grudgingly to the crew who flew her and complained that they didn't treat her with the consideration she deserved.

There was a current of tension beneath the casual conversation in the Control Office that night.

"What's the forecast?" someone asked.

"Medium cloud, north-west wind," Simon said.

"I can see a few stars through the cloud," Stephanie said, peering.

"It's supposed to be thicker over the target. They should have plenty of cover."

It would take four or five hours to fly to Kassel and back, so the Lancasters would not be back before two a.m. at the earliest. Kay knew the routines by now. Sometimes a plane would come back early if it developed a fault and had to jettison its bombs into the sea, or if it were badly damaged by a fighter before reaching the target. Unless this happened, or there was a Darky call from a stray plane from another station, there was little to do except wait. Kay helped Simon to go through his lines for the forthcoming revue, drank several cups of tea, talked to Stephanie about her fiancé's possible posting to the Middle East, and wondered whether she could possibly stay awake until eight in the morning. At uneventful times like this, in the early hours, the hands of the clock seemed to stop altogether . . .

A quarter to two. Slowly everyone's attention was focused on the dark blankness of the Control Office window, waiting for the radio loudspeaker to announce that the first returning bomber was crossing the coast. The station commander came in, as was his custom, to see the aircraft come back; the Flying Control Office was quite crowded at these times, in spite of the unsociable hour. Often there were several people standing up on the roof to watch the planes returning.

When at last the calls started coming in, Kay was relieved to have something to do, to slip into the routines. The runway lights were switched on as soon as the first aircraft to return, K-King, made contact.

"That's Sandy Beacham back," Simon said. "Must have gone all right. He doesn't sound too bothered."

Flight Lieutenant Beacham was the captain of one of the most experienced crews, just started on their second tour.

"I've never known Sandy sound bothered. It's just a bit of bus-driving as far as he's concerned," said Squadron Leader Bothwell. "No nerves at all."

The drone of the approaching Lancaster was soon joined by others, I-Item and J-Jig; these were told to join the circuit, stacked at 500-foot intervals, while Sandy Beacham in K-King made an immaculate landing. "K-King, ground flight to ground," were his final words, officially completing the flight.

"Venture J-Jig calling Blackrock. Venture J-Jig calling Blackrock. How do you receive? Over."

"Venture J-Jig, this is Blackrock," Kay replied. "Receiving strength niner. Over."

"Approaching airfield from coastline. Landing instructions please."

"Blackrock to Venture J-Jig, you are number three to land. Runway two-six, Wind ten m.p.h. Call on the downwind leg."

"Hello, Blackrock, Venture J-Jig downwind."

"Blackrock to Venture -J-Jig, you are clear to land," Kay said. "Reduce to one thousand feet . . ."

For each plane, Simon filled in the column on the board which showed the time of making R/T contact, and then the time of landing, under the heading "Pancake". The crews went straight in for debriefing, followed by a meal and bed. Sometimes, if they were anxious about friends in another aircraft, they came up to the Watch Office to wait with the others.

"Venture O-Orange calling Blackrock . . ."

"Join circuit at one thousand feet . . . Clear to land . . ."

The sky was filled with the noise of aircraft approaching and losing height; the roof of the Watch Office vibrated to the throb of the Merlin engines. One by one the details were filled in on the board. A-Able, Q-Queen, P-Peter . . . O-Orange landed awkwardly, bursting a tyre and skewing off the runway to finish lopsidedly near the place where the Darky plane had burst into flames; P-Peter had been holed, and her bomb aimer badly injured by flak. E-Easy, unharmed – "Charlie's kite made it there and back in one piece then. He'll be happy," Simon said. Occasionally, control staff glanced at the remaining gap on the board; nothing had been heard from T-Tare. The landed planes cleared the airfield, taxiing to dispersals where lorries waited to carry the crews back for interrogation. The watch office staff waited anxiously for T-Tare.

Simon checked the board. "Pilot Officer Wenham. Who's he?"

"New boy, on his first op," said Squadron Leader Bothwell. "The whole crew only came up yesterday from an O.T.U. The wireless ops have heard nothing from them since they crossed the enemy coast."

Nothing to do but wait: scanning the sky, ears straining for the faintest sound over the radio transmitter. Everyone knew what the casualty rates were: losses of three percent were at present considered average, with four percent or more not unusual. Three percent of tonight's whole force would be fifteen planes lost: a hundred and five airmen. With a sense of inevitability, Kay knew that T-Tare was not coming back. Gradually the expressions of everyone at the Control Bench changed from expectation to doubt, and then resignation.

Simon shook his head sadly. "He'd have run out of fuel by now."

"He could have made a forced landing somewhere else," Stephanie said.

They would probably never know, unless one of the other crews at debriefing reported seeing T-Tare shot down. T-Tare could have crashed in enemy territory, or exploded in mid-air, or plunged into the sea. Her crew might have parachuted to safety or been taken prisoner in Germany. Or she could have landed intact at another base a few miles away, in which case a phone call would soon be received to report the news. No one said much more about it. No one knew Pilot Officer Wenham or his crew anyway, so no one could feel any personal grief. Tomorrow morning an effects officer would sort through their belongings and clear their sleeping huts for another crew to use. A new Lancaster would be brought in and given the name of T-Tare. It was as if the name on the battle order had an existence quite independent of the plane itself or the men who flew her.

Kay filled in her log, trying not to remember the nervous new crews she had seen a few hours earlier, not to think of the seven families who would receive *Missing* telegrams next day. No telephone call came, so the plane was assumed lost. It was nothing out of the ordinary, just a routine night on ops.

"Good God, whatever do they put in this meat pie?" Felicity poked her fork through the thick pastry crust and speared a pink slab. "Has it ever been alive?"

Kay examined her own portion. "It's spam."

"I don't know how I'm not twelve stone by now, with all the stodge they give us."

"You needn't worry," Kay said. Felicity was as slim and elegant as ever. "Even though you never seem to go to PT sessions these days."

"Cunning arrangement of shifts," Felicity said. "Once was enough. It reminded me of school, with that hatchet-faced assistant section officer what's-her-name looking down her nose at me. It made me feel like a naughty second-former. Do they learn how to shrivel people up, as part of their training?"

"She's all right," Kay said. "I think she's a bit nervous, really. After all, she's only a year or two older than us. Here's your Canadian," she added as a cheerful group of aircrew came in at the cookhouse door.

Felicity glanced up. "Oh, I'm not seeing him any more."

"It's hard to keep up with you and your admirers. Who is it now, then?"

"Well—" Felicity leaned close. "Don't tell anyone, but I'm going out to dinner tonight with that divinely handsome officer from Intelligence."

"Really? The one who looks a bit like Errol Flynn?"

Felicity nodded smugly.

"But he's an *officer*," Kay said. "Not meant to socialise with low forms of life like us. What will happen if you get found out?"

"I'd get put on a charge, I suppose, and so would Ian. They're not likely to dismiss us, are they? Anyway, we'll take care not to get found out. Don't worry, I've got a very well-developed instinct."

"For avoiding trouble, or for getting into it?"

"I haven't been in much trouble yet, have I? I've been remarkably well-behaved. And we're not the only ones . . . you know that parachute packer, the one with gorgeous red hair—"

"Mind if I join you?" It was the curly-haired captain of A-Able, Sergeant Pilot Clifford, with a plateful of food. "You two girls look as if you could do with a bit of company."

"Not really," Felicity said. "We were just having a private conversation, actually."

Unabashed, Clifford sat down and began on his lunch. Although he was an experienced pilot, Kay thought he was probably only about twenty-two or -three. Aircrew of twenty-five or -six were considered to be on the elderly side: flying on ops soon turned young men into weathered veterans, so that there was an immense difference between the sprogs sent up from Operational Training Units and aircrew of Clifford's experience.

Clifford grinned at Kay and said, "Young Evans still hasn't forgiven me for pinching his partner at that dance the other night."

Felicity's instinct sharpened at once. "You mean that chap who was dancing with Kay? I thought he looked interested. Is he in your crew?"

"My navigator," Clifford said. "He's damned good. Oh, there he is – we're just back from flight testing. Ops again tonight. Over here, Evans boyo," he called.

David Evans made his way slowly through the tables and came to join them. He said hello to Kay, but apart from returning his greeting, she couldn't think of a single thing to say to him. She had the feeling that the meeting had been stage-managed by Clifford, especially when both he and Felicity finished their meal quickly and found some reason to leave the table. David continued eating his meat pie, not looking as if he was enjoying it much.

She had to say something. "You were on ops last night, weren't you?" was all she could think of. "I saw A-Able on the board."

He nodded. "And again tonight. It wasn't my first time, last night, but it was the longest distance, right across the Ruhr."

"Were you scared?"

His dark eyes scanned her face for a moment and then he nodded again, slowly. "I was terrified."

She guessed that he wouldn't have said so in front of his captain, but all the same she liked him for it. A lot of aircrew would have said no, it was a *good show* if it had gone well, or a *shaky do* if it hadn't, or would have been offended to be asked such a question at all.

"The good thing about being a navigator," he said, "is that you're busy all the time. You have to keep your mind on your maps and fixes, so you haven't got much time for thinking about the odds. Next to being pilot it's the best job."

"Sergeant Clifford said you were good. Damned good, were his actual words."

"Did he?" David looked so pleased that Kay guessed he had not received much praise directly from Clifford. "What's it like working at flying control? Do you like it?"

Kay told him about the tension of waiting for planes to return, and about not knowing what had happened to T-Tare.

"She was shot down over the target," David said bleakly. "We saw it. She was coned in the

96

searchlights and then a Junkers 88 got her. She went down in flames. No one bailed out."

He pushed his plate away, and Kay wished she hadn't mentioned it.

"Are you on tonight as well?" David asked.

"No, not after doing the night watch. I'm off until eight tomorrow morning. I'm not on night shift again till the day after."

"If I'm free tomorrow night," David said, "would you like to go into Lincoln? We could see a film, perhaps, or have a meal."

"That would be lovely," Kay said. She had wanted to tell him that she hadn't meant to go off with Clifford at the dance, but it no longer seemed necessary to explain. They arranged a meeting-point and left the cookhouse together, David heading for a few hours' sleep before briefing, and Kay to the concert hall for a re-hearsal with Stephanie and the third girl in the *Mikado* trio. Kay felt like skipping with excitement. Felicity would tease her later, she knew, but it was worth it.

CHRISTMAS

*I*t was a war film, a glossy naval adventure. The leading man was a squared-jawed commander who spent much of his time gazing across the sea with flinty eyes, occasionally barking out a curt command, and the women were either Wren officers with curvaceous figures or glamorous wives who mourned their men and wept shiny tears which didn't spoil their make-up.

"Sorry about that," David said as they left the Lincoln cinema. "I don't know who thinks people in wartime want war adventures for entertainment. Perhaps there'll be something better next week."

They talked about other films they had seen: *Gone with the Wind* and *For Whom the Bell Tolls*. It was a clear, starlit night, with the first hint of winter crispness. They each had a late pass, so there was no need to go straight back. Adjusting their eyes to the blackout they walked up the steep narrow streets to the Cathedral Close, where the twin towers of the west front were soaring pillars of solid black against a starry sky.

"I usually see it from the air, at dawn," David said, "like our own special beacon, guiding us home."

They had heard the drone of heavy bombers flying overhead while they were in the cinema, aircraft from a base further inland setting out for Germany. Lincolnshire was so densely clustered with airfields that it must be rare for the local residents to sleep undisturbed; it took heavy fog over the bases to keep the aircraft grounded. Kay wanted to ask David more about flying on ops, but she thought of all the *Careless Talk* posters of Hitler and Goering sitting behind chatterers on buses or hiding in bar room wallpaper. Everyone was constantly being warned not to discuss the work of the station when off the premises.

David pointed out various constellations, which he had learned as part of his training as a navigator. "See that little cluster there? That's Pleiades."

Kay looked. "Isn't that funny? You can see more stars there if you look to one side rather than straight at them."

"It's something to do with the way the light strikes the back of your eye, I think," David said. "How many can you see? Most people's eyesight isn't good enough to see more than seven."

The group of distant stars was like a handful of silver dust thrown against the blackness. Kay tried to count, but the individual pinpoints of light danced and faded, and merged into a smudge of light.

"Come on, you're getting cold," David said. "Are you hungry? Shall we see if we can get some supper before we go back? I think there's a place near here that stays open late."

Kay felt foolish at having spent most of the day worrying about the evening out. What would they talk about, she had wondered, what would David think of her, how was she expected to behave? She would have liked to ask Felicity for advice, but did not want to admit that she had never been out alone with a boy before; Felicity would laugh at her, and think her ludicrously childish. Now, in spite of her doubts, she was in no hurry for the evening to end. David took her hand as they walked along the narrow street, and said, as if he needed to justify it, "So that neither of us falls over in the dark," and she realised that he felt a little awkward, too.

They went to an informal restaurant not far

from the cathedral. It was dominated by air force uniforms, so that the room seemed awash in a sea of blue, varied by one tableful of American olive. A gramophone in one corner played jazz music, competing with conversation and laughter to create an atmosphere of warmth and relaxation. Some acquaintances of David's waved at him to come and join them, but he steered Kay instead to a table for two by the blacked-out window. Someone wolf-whistled, and she guessed that David would be teased about being seen with her when he returned to camp.

While they ate, they talked about David's training in Canada and Scotland and Kay's holidays in Ireland, and she told him about her mother's work in London, and about her father and his paintings.

"Maybe you've inherited his talent?" David suggested.

Kay shook her head. "Not at all. I don't think I've got any talent for anything. What about you? Are you artistic?"

David said that he was hopeless at drawing but wanted to be a photographer, and that he was practising with a camera in his off-duty hours. "Mainly aircraft at the moment, for lack of the chance to do much else. It's not really allowed, but a lot of people do it. Apart from that I like landscapes. Mountains, in particular."

"That's like my father," Kay said. She described for him the paintings in Uncle Jack's apple loft, and David said that he would love to see them.

When they got back to camp he kissed her in what she imagined to be a brotherly fashion, not at all like the passionate moonlit embraces they had seen in the film. Felicity would no doubt have considered this rather tame, but Kay thought it perfectly appropriate. David said that he hoped she would go out with him again, and she was happy with that.

Charlie Fox had got hold of some lengths of parachute silk and had persuaded one of the meteorology WAAFs to dye them and paint them with oriental lilies. Kay, Stephanie and the third girl, Joyce, a tall fair girl who worked as a clerk, designed a simple kimono pattern and spent their spare time sewing them. With these, they were to wear wigs made of black horsehair which were itchy to wear, but looked effective when coiled up into topknots and skewered with broken-off knitting needles. Charlie had even managed to get proper theatrical make-up and for the performance the three girls had oriental complexions, rosebud mouths and elongated eyes. Kay looked at her reflection in the dressing-room mirror and hardly recognised herself.

Stephanie went up to the wings and peeped

round the heavy curtain. "There's quite a big audience," she reported. "Only a few empty seats left, at the back. Even the station commander's come along, and the Queen Bee!"

Kay had never realised before how awful stage fright was. Her throat felt so tight that she felt sure she wouldn't be able to get a single note out. Taking a peep herself, she saw David in the fifth row from the front, between Felicity and Bob Clifford. He had promised to come along if he could. She felt ridiculously pleased, even more determined to put on her best performance. The station commander was sitting next to the WAAF CO in the second row, both looking as serious as if they were attending a meeting at the Air Ministry rather than a light-hearted camp entertainment.

The revue began with Charlie on the piano, playing a medley of popular songs; he was an excellent pianist, and could play anything by ear. Next came Wally, one of the mess staff, as a comically inept juggler who stood as if rooted to the spot with panic while his arms shot out like the tentacles of an octopus to grab flying beer bottles. Various comments and insults mingled with applause from the audience. In the wings, Kay licked her lips anxiously and then wondered whether she had smudged her lipstick. Joyce, who sang in the choir and was going to sing some Vera Lynn songs in the second half, was ready to lead on, not nervous at all. Wally's applause died away, and Charlie began to play the bouncy opening bars of the Gilbert and Sullivan piece. The three girls minced on to the stage with shuffling steps and bowed to the audience, elbows out and palms together.

"Three little maids from school are we,
Pert as a schoolgirl well can be,
Filled to the brim with girlish glee –
Three little maids from school . . ."

Kay found that her voice was working after all, rising in reasonable tune with the others. She remembered the words for her short Pitti-Sing solo, and her nerves disappeared as she saw from the smiling faces in front of her that the audience was appreciative. In the intervals between verses, all three singers pretended to whisper outrageous secrets, giggling girlishly with hands to mouths; Kay knew that the effect was made comic by the fact that Joyce, at five foot ten, towered above Stephanie and herself. She caught sight of Charlie's grinning face as he played, and knew that it wasn't just her imagination – the performance was going better than ever before.

"Three little maids who all unwary
Come from a ladies' seminary,
Free from its genius tutelary –
Three little maids from school,

Three little mai – ds from school."

As Charlie rattled off the final bars, the three left the stage in demure procession, then had to shuffle back on again to receive their applause.

More than one voice was shouting, "Encore! Encore!" and even the station commander was clapping vigorously. Joyce went over and whispered to Charlie, and they performed the final verse again – they had nothing else in their repertoire. Kay rather wished they had. She could take to theatrical life, she decided.

Charlie hugged each of them as they came off. "Terrific, girls. They loved it."

Mike took over at the piano after the interval while Charlie went off to get changed for an act of his own, which no one had been allowed to see in rehearsal. After Joyce's songs and Simon's narrative poem, Mike began to play a typical silent film accompaniment, with tripping rises and rolling crescendos. After a few moments Charlie waddled on to the stage as Charlie Chaplin, with bemused expression and Hitler moustache, his foxy hair hidden beneath a straggly black wig. He played Charlie Chaplin as a Home Guard, with armband, rifle, tin helmet and respirator case. Encumbered by all this gear he tried to put on first the gas mask and then a parachute pack, his face registering various stages of helpless frustration. In his silent contortions he managed to pull the whole parachute out, and ended up so hopelessly entangled that he had to be dragged off the stage by Simon.

"That was brilliant, Charlie," Kay whispered to him in the wings as he extricated himself. "You're wasted on aircraft – you ought to be a professional entertainer."

Charlie, still being Charlie Chaplin, mimed being overcome with bashfulness. Kay, giggling, had to be pushed out of the way as the final "chorus-girl" act clomped past to the stage. This was a line-up of ground crew in drag parodying the Cochran girls' London act, all prancing out of time and kicking each other by mistake and losing their wigs. Shouts, wolf-whistles and insults resounded from the mostly male audience as the troupe lurched and thrashed about. To finish, there were more popular songs, with the audience joining in this time.

The concert had been a success. Most of the audience drifted off towards the mess bars; David came up with Bob Clifford and Felicity to congratulate Kay on her performance.

"You're a dark horse, telling me you had no talent," David said. "I'd no idea you could sing like that—"

"You don't share a billet with her," Felicity said. "I've had *Three Little Maids from School* till I could recite it in my sleep. You were terrific, though, Kay."

"Are you sure you know which one was me, behind all this make-up?"

"It looked like fun. I wish I'd made the effort to join in," Felicity said.

"Lovely costume," Bob Clifford said, leering at Kay. "Makes a nice change to see girls out of uniform." He made a show of smoothing his hair back and straightening his collar. "Now, if you'll excuse me, I must go and sweet-talk one of those gorgeous girls from the chorus line . . ."

Afterwards, there was a brief party for the participants behind stage. The station commander appeared briefly to compliment them on putting on a show despite unexpected postings, difficult shift combinations and various minor crises. Charlie was already talking about a new project: he wanted to put on a whole play.

"I don't think I'm going to be in anything with you again, Charlie; you're such a show-stealer," Joyce said.

"You don't mean it." Charlie put on his sad-clown face. "What about you, Kay? You won't let me down, will you?"

"That depends what you're thinking of doing," Kay said. But she thought she would take part, if it were possible. The revue had been fun, the rehearsals as much as the performance.

*   *   *

"Ask me again," Felicity said, pressing her knuckles against her eyes with the effort of remembering.

"All right." Kay had her gen-book full of diagrams and notes open on her lap. "What kind of flux would you use with stainless steel?"

"Hydrochloric acid."

"Yes. And for copper?"

"Tallow – no, I mean water-white rosin and turpentine. Is that the one? Oh, Kay, I'll never remember it all. This bit isn't too bad, but all that about inductance and resistance . . ."

The first exam for the trainee R/T operators was held just before Christmas. In spite of Felicity's doubts, the pass list on the Waafery notice board a few days later gave her name as well as Kay's. Now they were entitled to sew "sparks" badges on their sleeves, like the ones the wireless operators wore. They were still Aircraftwoman Second Class in rank, but could now drop the u/t prefix which had marked them as novices.

David was promoted to Flight Sergeant a few days later, and he and Kay went out for a meal in Lincoln to celebrate. She did not realise that Charlie Fox had seen them on the bus coming back until the next evening, when she had offered to help him sort through the muddle of costumes and props in the theatre changing room. They had been talking about something else entirely when Charlie suddenly said, "You want to be careful about getting yourself too involved with aircrew, Kay."

"Oh—" Kay was taken aback, even though she knew Charlie must have had ample opportunity to see her with David at the camp cinema or in the NAAFI. "I'm not involved with *aircrew*," she countered, "not in general, that is . . ."

"No, I know. I mean your particular airman. Saw you on the late bus back from Lincoln the other night," Charlie explained.

Kay felt herself blushing, to her annoyance. She and David had sat on the back seat on the way home; it had been dark, of course, so Charlie could hardly have seen more than them getting on and off.

"I'm sorry, I didn't see you. You should have come over and said hello," she said.

Charlie gave her a wry look. "Didn't want to play gooseberry, did I? Be careful with that helmet, it's got rough edges."

"What's wrong with aircrew?" she said defensively, putting the helmet on a shelf.

"Nothing wrong with them." Charlie held up a papier-mâché mask and examined it from several angles. "What I mean is, don't build up heartache for yourself. They're here today, gone tomorrow, aircrew are. Your young man seems a very nice chap, but he could be posted away next week. You know the rest of his crew have nearly finished their tour."

"David isn't my young man," Kay protested.

"Oh, no," Charlie said drily. "It doesn't look like it."

Kay was getting used to offers of advice from Mike and Simon in the Control Office, who seemed to feel a protective responsibility towards the young WAAFs they worked with; Charlie was younger than them, only four years or so older than Kay, but he too seemed to be assuming an uncle-like duty towards her. "You be careful about going to those dances," Mike had warned her once; "some of those glamour boys would eat you for breakfast, given half a chance." He made them sound like dangerous predatory animals. Felicity would doubtless have given a sharp retort if any such advice had come her way, but Kay realised that it was kindly meant. The camaraderie among the ground staff, the more-or-less permanent residents of the station, could not easily include aircrew, because of the different nature of their duties. Kay did not worry about any threat from the "glamour boys", but David being posted away was a distinct possibility, one they had discussed. And she was well aware that a posting was not the worst thing that could happen. "Here today, gone tomorrow" covered worse possibilities, as Charlie had been hinting. She glanced at him, but he said no more on the subject, and held up a crumpled Father Christmas jacket trimmed with cotton wool.

"One of the squadron leaders made this last year, can you believe it? I suppose we'll be needing it again soon, if the mice haven't got at it too badly."

The imminent posting did not happen, after all. Just before Christmas, Clifford's crew finished their first tour of thirty ops and were stood down for a rest, while David was to transfer to another crew in B Flight whose navigator was going into hospital for a minor operation. David would have leave over Christmas and New Year, followed by two weeks away on a radar course, and then he would return to fly on ops with Flight Lieutenant Beacham's crew in K-King. He said that he would ask for it to be renamed K-Kay.

Kay told Felicity about the changes. "At least he's going to be with an experienced crew again. Sandy Beacham's supposed to be completely unflappable. And they're already on his second tour."

She was relieved that David was not flying on ops at present: night raids were going to Berlin several times a week, with heavy losses. New crews on arrival at the station were being sent straight out on the long journey to Berlin and back in midwinter conditions, without the easing-in of a few routine minelaying raids. Not surprisingly, several failed to return. Kay was getting used to the blank spaces on the board, the low-key "Shame about so-and-so", which was often the only acknowledgement. It seemed to her to be an amazing squandering of lives, not far removed from the wholesale slaughter on the Somme and around Ypres in the last war. The crews hated going to Berlin, she knew, with the long flight over enemy territory and the fierce defences. She hoped that the focus would shift elsewhere before David returned to flying duties.

Felicity said that Kay was silly to stick to just one boyfriend. "You ought to take the chance to go out with other people when he goes away on that course. There's no shortage."

"But I don't want to," Kay said.

Felicity was lying on her bed filing her nails. "You'll end up disappointed. David could be posted away after all, or . . . well, anything could happen."

First Charlie, now Felicity, Kay thought. Why does everyone want to give me advice?

"It's not as if you've had many boyfriends," Felicity continued. "You ought to play the field a bit."

"But I don't want to play the field. I like David."

"For all you know, he might go out with other girls," Felicity pointed out. "He's got to do something while you're on evening duties."

"There's no reason why he shouldn't," Kay said, although surprised to find how much she disliked the idea. But she didn't think David did. He had mentioned a former girlfriend in Canada who had written to him recently, but that was all.

"He's asked me to go to Monmouth with him over New Year," she said. "I've got leave. But I want to go home and see Mum as well."

Felicity sighed, as if giving Kay up as a hopeless case. "Oh, God. It is serious then. Clifford told me he was crazy about you."

"Who, Clifford?" Kay said, stalling. "I wouldn't have thought I was his type at all."

"No, I meant David is, idiot."

Kay considered this. Gratifying though it was, she was not sure that she liked being gossiped about by Clifford.

"It doesn't necessarily mean it's serious, just because he's invited me home," she said. "You make it sound like a case of pneumonia. Anyway – do you think I ought to go?"

"Meet Mummy and Daddy? It'll be an engagement ring next. Well, you know what I think." Felicity held out a hand with fingers splayed and examined the pointed nails from several angles. "Let him know there are other fish in the sea. Of course he's very nice and all that, I can see why you're so keen, but I'd keep him at arm's length if I were you. Metaphorically, at any rate."

"Oh? Like you do with Ian?" Kay mocked.

"That's different," Felicity said airily, starting on the other hand. "We're both mature, sophisticated people . . . familiar with the ways of the world . . ."

Kay hurled a pillow at her. She decided to ignore Felicity's advice. To Felicity, a relationship with a boyfriend was either casual and fun, or serious enough to lead to marriage, or an intense burst of passion which would quickly fizzle out as soon as the next attractive man came along. Kay thought that her relationship with David didn't fit any of those categories; it was friendship, and conversation, and understanding, and attraction . . . all sorts of things. Was there enough to be labelled "serious", like a hospital diagnosis? Kay wasn't sure.

She wrote to Alice to make arrangements for a visit home. She would be on duty over Christmas, but was due for nearly a week's leave over New Year and the first few days of January. David had leave for the whole of the Christmas period, so they had four days in the middle which coincided. Not at all sure how her mother would react, Kay mentioned David's invitation to Monmouth. Much to her surprise, Alice wrote back saying, *Yes, do go to Wales for New Year. If you'd like to bring your friend here to stay for a night or two, I'd be very pleased to have him. It will be rather cramped but I'm sure we can manage.*

"What do you think of this?" Kay said, and read the letter to Felicity. "Mum suggesting that I actually bring David into the house, a member of Bomber Command aircrew?"

"Why not?" Felicity said airily. "Let her see that he's a perfectly ordinary human being, not some fiendish Hun-hater."

"Well . . ." Kay said. "I don't really see how she could dislike him."

"Of course she won't. It won't be an ordeal unless you make it one. You always worry too much."

Eventually it was agreed that David would come to London for the night of the 29th, and that they would travel to Monmouth together on the following day. There would be time for Kay to return to London for another two days before reporting back, while David went off to Wing, in Buckinghamshire, for his course. David seemed quite happy with the arrangements, and Kay wished she didn't feel so anxious.

Felicity found a new way of breaking the

rules. She had arranged to go to a Christmas dance in Lincoln with Ian and was determined to wear her evening dress, which she had asked her mother's housekeeper to send on from home.

"I'm sick of dances in uniform, and it is Christmas. I need a bit of glamour."

Kay admired the confection of aquamarine tulle, spangled with brilliants. She could imagine how gorgeous Felicity would look in it. It was strictly forbidden to have civilian clothes on the camp, let alone wear them, but Felicity was up to the challenge. Kay watched her getting ready for the evening out.

"I should think Ian will be bowled over," Kay said, when Felicity had done her hair and make-up and had put on the dress, "unless he looks at your feet."

Below the full-skirted flounces of the aquamarine hem, Felicity's ankles and feet were staidly clad in grey lisle stockings and black lace-up shoes.

Felicity looked down at her legs and giggled. "It does look ridiculous. But it's all part of the plan." She showed Kay a small case which contained her silk stockings, evening shoes, make-up and hairbrush. She put on her greatcoat and buttoned it up to the neck. "There. A perfectly turned-out, dutiful little WAAF – till I get to Lincoln. No one will guess."

Felicity's luck held, and she got away with it. For Kay, there were no off-camp excursions; she was on duty in Flying Control until four o'clock on Christmas Eve. There was not much flying, and the phone rang several times with drunken messages from the Officers' Mess – including a request for landing permission for S-Santa and R-Reindeer. After her duty, Kay went to a dance in the Sergeants' Mess; David had gone home to Wales, but she followed Felicity's advice sufficiently to dance with several different partners.

On Christmas Day itself there was a tradition that the officers served the other ranks their Christmas dinner before having their own meal. All the usual *Careless Talk* and *Dig for Victory* posters in the mess were hidden behind streamers and bunting, and there was even a Christmas tree. Officers went from table to table with jugs of beer to top up glasses and high spirits. The cooks had somehow defied wartime austerity to provide a four-course meal, with plenty of second helpings for those who could find room for more. Ian, Felicity's intelligence officer, was serving at the next table. Kay scrutinised him discreetly. Yes, he was handsome, in a flawless, matinée idol sort of way, and obviously knew it. The pair of WAAFs he was assiduously looking after had gone all pink and giggly, and Kay did not think it was just the alcohol. He and Felicity were not acknowledging each other at all.

Through a slightly alcoholic haze Kay noticed Felicity flirting energetically with Flight Lieutenant Beacham. She supposed this was a diversionary tactic, rather like a spoof raid, and watched Sandy Beacham with interest as he went to and fro with servings of plum pudding. He had impassive features in a hollow-cheeked face, and pale blue eyes which rested occasionally on Felicity in surprise. He was supposed to be unassailable by flak or Messerschmitts, but Kay wondered whether he was quite so impervious to the full onslaught of Felicity's charm.

Later, there was a film and dancing and a lavish high tea, and at midnight Kay retired to Flying Control for her night watch, seriously deprived of sleep and glad that the eight hours ahead promised to be uneventful. Tonight, at least, there would be no blank spaces on the board, no bombers over Berlin.

DAVID

*A*ll Kay's balanced reasoning about David vanished the moment she saw him come through the ticket barrier at Paddington station. He came straight to her and kissed her, in a very unbrotherly way, and hugged her tightly and said in her ear, "I've been so looking forward to seeing you. It seems like ages," and she hugged him back and felt slightly dizzy. Someone clucked at them irritably, trying to get through to the train. They broke apart and looked at each other.

David said, "I like your hair loose like that. You look different in civvies."

"So do you. Nice."

He laughed, and picked up his bag. "We'd better get out of everyone's way."

They went by tube train to east London.

People clutching blankets and possessions were already settling down on the underground platforms, as they had done since the Blitz. Workers returning by the early evening trains crowded the stairways and pavements, and late shoppers were still queuing outside the butcher's blacked-out door. Kay took David down the narrow street towards the flat, where tall buildings seemed to block out what little light remained. Although she had been at home since yesterday she had still not readjusted to the cramped surroundings and the crowded streets and shops; after the sweep of airfield and the big Lincolnshire sky, she felt hemmed in. She wondered what David, used to Monmouth, would think of the area she lived in and her mother's tiny flat. He might think it a slum; Felicity undoubtedly would.

Alice, who must have heard them opening the shared front door of the flats, stood at the top of the stairs to greet them. Kay led the way up, desperately anxious that David and her mother should like each other. This was a new experience for her and she was not sure how to handle it. She hoped it would handle itself.

"Mum, this is David. David, Mum," she said awkwardly.

Alice held out her hand, smiling, and then Kay saw a fractional hesitation, accompanied by a sharp intake of breath as if she had seen something unexpected. Then she seemed to recover, shaking David's hand warmly.

"I'm very pleased to meet you, Mrs Leary," David said. Kay knew that he had noticed her mother's reaction.

"I'm glad you could come," Alice said, regaining her composure. "Do come in. I'm in the middle of cooking . . ."

Kay wondered what had surprised her mother. Perhaps she had expected some thick-skinned, flak-happy "Brylcreem boy"? Well, David was nothing like that: Kay wouldn't have dared to introduce such a character into their home, even in the unlikely event of wanting to. Her mother made David welcome, and they were soon chatting easily, interrupted by frequent exits to the kitchen to tend to the cooking. Alice had managed to get a small joint for a roast dinner, and had even made a passable Christmas pudding with what fruit and sugar she had been able to get; Kay guessed that she had been hoarding food over the past few weeks to prepare for this leave, and felt rather guilty when she thought of the lavish spread at the Mess dinner. Alice had been working over Christmas and had probably made do with a sandwich.

David had brought a present for Alice, a framed photograph of the River Wye at Symonds Yat. As it happened, Kay's present to her mother was a pair of framed watercolours of Lincoln, so Alice immediately took down the faded old pictures she had hung around the room to replace Patrick's, and put the three new ones up, saying that they made an instant improvement. Kay gave David a thick scarf to wear on winter ops, and a little black china cat for a good luck charm, and a book of poems by Gerard Manley Hopkins. He gave her a book, too, about the west coast of Ireland, but said that she would have to wait for the other part of her present until they got to Monmouth.

After dinner they all did the washing- and drying-up together in the narrow kitchen, dodging and side-stepping each other, and then listened to a concert on the wireless and talked until late. All evening Kay felt aware of David in a new and exciting way, her eyes following him, noticing the taut slimness of his body as he stood to adjust one of the pictures, the quick alertness of his dark eyes, which seemed to miss nothing, and the muscled length of his thigh as he sat forward in his chair. He had a natural grace which made all his movements attractive. She wanted him to kiss her again the way he had at the station; she wanted to be alone with him, but at the same time she wanted to see her esteem of him reflected in her mother's approval. She was amazed at herself, at this sudden welling-up of feeling. She had always thought of herself as sensible and under control. This was rather like being drunk, she imagined; the feeling of being swept along by some strange force, feet not quite on the ground.

She had made up a camp bed in her mother's room so that David could have her bed. When they retired, at about half-past one, Alice kissed Kay and said softly, so that David should not hear through the thin wall, "I like him very much, dear. And you obviously have a great deal in common. I'm glad you brought him home."

"I hoped you'd like him. And thank you for a lovely evening. But why did you look at him like that, at first?"

Alice picked up her hairbrush and turned to the mirror, her back to Kay.

"He reminded me of someone, that was all," she said. "Just for a moment."

Kay would have liked to ask who, but her mother's manner discouraged further questioning. She curled up for sleep on the camp bed, pleased that the evening had gone well. All the same, she knew that there was one topic which had carefully been avoided, and which David's presence had to some extent excluded – the bombing raids on Berlin. Alice had said nothing about the subject at all, even before David had arrived. Kay could guess what restraint that had taken.

Next day Kay and David travelled by train to Monmouth. David's parents lived in a small terraced house near the river. They were rather older than Kay's mother, obviously very proud of their son and his achievements, and ready to welcome Kay as one of the family. David showed her the darkroom he had made in a garden shed, and some of his photographs, which she admired.

"You must take some pictures of Kay while she's here," Mrs Evans said over supper.

David said that he planned to.

"Now, what about this dance tomorrow night at the Town Hall? You two ought to take the chance to go."

"Would you like to go, Kay?" David said. "It would be fun, for New Year's Eve."

"But I haven't got anything to wear," Kay said.

"What you've got on looks perfectly all right to me."

"Don't be silly, dear," Mrs Evans said. "Of course she'd need to have a proper dance frock. It's quite a smart occasion."

"Well, what can we do? It would be a pity to miss it. Can't we borrow something? I suppose I should have mentioned it while we were in London. I didn't really think about clothes."

"I haven't got an evening dress, anyway," Kay said. She had never been to a formal dance.

"Oh, we must get you there somehow," Mrs Evans said, as if she were Kay's fairy godmother. She thought for a moment. "I know, I'll ask Mrs Johns, up on Raglan Road. She's got three daughters who are always going to parties and dances, and two of them are away in the Wrens. I'm sure we can fix you up." She looked Kay up and down. "You're only a little thing, aren't you? Still, we could always take up a hem. I'll go up and see Mrs Johns tomorrow."

Kay had been given David's room; he would have to sleep on the sofa downstairs. She looked around at his belongings. A couple of flimsy model aircraft, childishly painted; a framed photograph of a mountain landscape; shelves of fiction and books about photography and aviation; old school text books on physics and geometry. It interested her to see him in a different setting, to learn more about him. Like her, he was an only child.

Next day, she and David caught a bus to Hay-on-Wye and walked up towards Gospel Pass, in the Black Mountains. Kay loved the wildness of the scenery, so different from the level plain around Lincoln. They followed a narrow road through sheep-grazed turf and bog grasses; the Black Mountains rose ahead, purple smudges against thick shifting cloud. There were streaks of snow on the high summits. A cold wind gusted, encouraging brisk walking.

"This is one of the real bonuses of leave," David said, buttoning up his top collar, "to be able to walk and talk, miles away from anyone. Air force life has its good points, but privacy isn't one of them."

He talked a little about flying on ops, about the special demands of winter flying, and the dangers of icing cloud. Kay always wanted to hear him talk about flying, so that she could more clearly imagine his experiences next time he went.

"Does it get easier?" she asked. "Less frightening, more a matter of routine?"

"In some ways. But I don't think I shall ever get blasé about it, no matter how many times I go."

"I suppose everyone's scared, if they're honest."

"Most of the chaps don't talk about it much. Talking makes it worse. But I think you *ought* to be scared, as long as you don't let it take over. It keeps your wits about you."

Kay thought of Sandy Beacham. "Your new pilot's supposed to have no nerves at all."

"Then I'd say he's either a very good actor, or he's got no imagination."

"Do you think you'll get on all right with the new crew?"

David splashed through a puddle. "I don't know yet. Beacham seems very difficult to get to know. And there's Isaacs, the bomb aimer – he's Jewish, with relatives in Poland. Or at least he *had* relatives in Poland. He doesn't know whether they survived the Luftwaffe raids on Warsaw. Now all he wants to do is kill Germans. I suppose it's understandable to want revenge, with all the rumours of what's happening to Jews in Germany. For most people, it's just a job."

Kay knew from her own conversations with aircrew that most of them did not talk about killing Germans. They were too much concerned with their own survival, and the safe return of others in their Flight.

"My mother said that in the last war, the troops didn't hate the Germans at all," Kay said. "They were all in it together, facing the same awful conditions. If they hated anyone, it was their own generals."

"I met some German aircrew once," David said. "They were shot down when I was at Air Observer School in Scotland. One of them spoke English and he was perfectly friendly, as if we were colleagues who happen to be on different sides."

"But we're doing awful things to the German civilians. Mum says it's no different from the Luftwaffe bombing London."

"Well, it isn't," David said. "I'm glad not to have been on any of the Berlin raids. When I

127

was training, we were practising low-level flying to drop supplies and agents for the Maquis in France. That was what I wanted to do. I was disappointed when I was taken off it and posted up to Windersby."

"So what sort of targets have you been told about at the briefings?"

"All the ops I've been on so far, it's been oil terminals, shipyards, munition factories, things like that. Legitimate targets, or at least that's what they tell us."

"Are the Berlin raids different?" It was not something Kay liked to think about. "What do they say at the briefings for those?"

"I don't know," David said. "And I hope I don't find out."

A bunch of panicking sheep ran along the track ahead of them for a few moments before plunging into a dip. Kay said, "Do you think it will end the war, if we keep on bombing Berlin? Now that the Russians are advancing and the Allies are gaining ground in Italy?"

David shrugged. "I've heard that Air Marshall Harris is predicting surrender by April, if we carry on pounding Berlin at this rate."

"Four more months."

"If he's not being over-optimistic. But it's costly. As you know."

Kay nodded, thinking of the aircraft letters removed from the blackboard with one wipe of a cloth. But David was pursuing a different train of thought.

"The truth is, you're so worried about dropping the bombs and clearing out before the fighters get you that it's easy to forget what's happening on the ground." He thrust his hands more deeply into his coat pockets. "But it's always there, in the back of my mind. Especially because I know damn well that any small mathematical error on my part, any slight miscalculation, can decide whether someone underneath lives or dies . . . It seems so cold-blooded, sitting there in the clouds with my gauges and charts, like playing God with people's lives . . ."

"You shouldn't think of it like that. It's not really your responsibility. You're just carrying out orders."

David shook his head, and Kay knew that he was right; it would be easier for him if he did not worry, but not more creditable.

"The question is, I suppose," he said, "what can bring about the greatest good for the greatest number – what's that called? Utilitarianism, or something? If Hitler can be forced to surrender, and the outcome is better for hundreds of thousands of people in Europe, the Jews and the Poles, can that be set against the lives of civilians in Berlin who are being killed to bring that about?"

They talked for a while about whether the

end could justify the means. Neither was sure, and their conversation led them into confusing philosophical realms far removed from the everyday life they knew on a bomber station, where the main concern was to see everyone safely back from the night's ops.

On their return they found that David's mother had devoted much of her day to out-fitting Kay for the New Year's Eve dance. She showed them a dress of white patterned silk, with tight elbow-length sleeves and a full skirt. There were shoes to match, loaned by a differ-ent daughter who shared Kay's shoe size, and an evening bag studded with imitation pearls. Kay thought she wouldn't dare to wear the dress for fear of ripping the skirt or spilling something down the front, but Mrs Evans was so delighted with the result that it was worth the risk. As her only jewellery, Kay wore the heart-shaped gold locket necklace which David had given her the previous evening as a Christ-mas present. She had put it on straightaway and said that she would wear it always.

Having no other warm coat, she had to wear her uniform greatcoat over the dress.

"Come on then, Cinderella." David, in his best blue, offered her his arm. "Just you be careful after midnight."

"Are you afraid I'll turn back into a WAAF?"

David's parents waved them off and prepared to see the New Year in with a glass or two of whisky and the Home Service. Outside it was bitterly cold, with frost glittering on the pavement in the low beam of David's torch. Kay's feet slithered in the flimsy shoes.

"Do you remember the first year of the blackout," she said, "when you weren't allowed to have even a torch, and people used to trip up on pavements and bump into trees and then apologise to them?"

"Yes! I remember getting completely lost in Gloucester one night and then falling over some builders' scaffolding into a trench. I've still got a scar to prove it. Just stop there for a moment." He grabbed her arm, so that she thought there was some unseen obstacle in their path.

"What?"

"I just wanted to tell you," he said, "before we get there, that you look beautiful."

She giggled. "In the pitch dark?"

"No, seriously. You do." He tried to kiss her, fumbling in the dark so that their noses bumped at first and they both giggled, and then his arms tightened around her and the urge to laugh disappeared in the intensity of the kiss. She wondered whether David felt the same as she did, the last few days: as if a comfortable liking for each other had suddenly turned into

131

something else, a new heightening of feeling.

"It'll be New Year before we get to the dance, at this rate." His mouth was against her ear, his breath warm. He smelled of shaving soap.

"I don't care. I want you all to myself."

"You can have me all to yourself. You'll be the only person there as far as I'm concerned."

Reluctantly, they left the intimate darkness for the gaiety of the Town Hall. It was a suitably festive occasion, with a Christmas tree and draped bunting, and a dance band, and someone important in a gold chain of office; the floor was already filled with swaying couples. David introduced Kay to several acquaintances, but danced only with her. Kay was light-headed with music and love; the lights and the coloured dresses and David's face whirled round as they danced. At midnight there was a silence in the hall while everyone listened to the chiming of the town clock, and then Auld Lang Syne and more dancing.

It was 1944.

ALICE

Alice saw in the New Year on her own, with a glass of sherry and the wireless, and the black cat sitting on her lap. She had spent part of the evening at the home of friends from work, but had come home early, intending to go to bed as soon as she had heard the chimes of midnight. She was used to her own company and she was not sure that the New Year would bring much worth celebrating, unless it could see an end to the war.

Today's *Times* lay folded on the dining table, showing the headline "MORE AREAS OF BERLIN WRECKED". The German capital had been bombarded mercilessly over the past two months, with a token break for Christmas. From what Alice read in the papers, there no longer seemed to be a pretence that

German civilians were regarded as anything other than military targets. "The Battle of Berlin", the newspaper called it. Battle! Alice threw a scornful glance at the headline. Defenceless men, women and children against high explosives and incendiary bombs: what sort of battle was that? "Beyond the official statement that high explosives and incendiaries were dropped in residential areas, no messages have been allowed to mention the extent of the damage," she read. It was hard to get at the truth behind the journalistic distortions, but Alice had seen enough of the Blitz to imagine for herself what it must be like in Berlin at the moment. And Bomber Command was perfecting the techniques of aerial bombardment, so that the Luftwaffe raids on London already looked outdated: an ever-increasing tonnage of bombs was pouring almost nightly from forces of aircraft hundreds strong. A thousand strong, in the raid on Cologne . . .

Alice lifted the lid of her writing desk and took out a framed photograph. A woman in her forties, simply dressed: Hanni Böckler, from Hamburg. Alice had met her on a visit to Germany with her friend Lorna, two years after the last Armistice. They had become friends, never suspecting that their two countries would be at war again within their own lifetimes, and had corresponded ever since. Hanni's young husband had been killed in the Great War, leaving her with two small children, and she had gone to Hamburg soon afterwards to find work.

Alice wondered how long it would be before she could find out whether Hanni had survived the firestorm of Hamburg.

And now Kay was working on a bomber station, and so was Stephen. Stephen might have flown on the raid to Hamburg, for all she knew . . . She hated to think about it.

Because she was a widow, and Kay an only child, Alice had always been very careful not to be over-possessive. She would not try to run Kay's life for her, determined to let her make her own decisions and form her own opinions. But she had had to hide her dismay when Kay had written to tell her of her posting. She could understand the attractions of the WAAF, the glamour and excitement of working on an operational station. War made it an exciting time to be young, in many ways. But it grieved her to think of all the other wartime occupations Kay could have chosen. Of all things, to have ended up in the one place Alice had most feared, a bomber station . . .

Kay had not said much, but enough for Alice to form an idea of what it must be like to be involved in that one specialised corner of the war. Understandably, Kay's thoughts were tied up with the people she knew, the young men who risked their lives on dangerous missions over Germany, and whose courage could not be doubted. Especially so, now that she had a boy-friend. And Alice had to admit that she was reassured by David; he was far from the gung-ho, over-confident types she had feared Kay might become involved with. She should have trusted Kay's judgement. David was a thoughtful, intelligent young man, well-suited to Kay. They were so obviously in love, unable to keep their eyes off each other, that they had brought a kind of glow into the room with them. Well, Kay was very young, and Alice knew from her own youth how quickly ro-mance could flourish under wartime condi-tions. It might not last, but at least David didn't seem at all the type to take advantage of Kay's inexperience. Seeing them together had brought back sharp, sweet memories of herself and Patrick, herself and Edward . . .

Alice thought again of the first shock of seeing David coming up the narrow stairway. The light had been dim, and as soon as he had entered the flat she had seen that he wasn't really like Edward at all. Edward had had blue eyes, David's were dark; Edward had been taller, with a thinner face and curly hair. It was just her memory playing tricks, as it sometimes did, even after all these years. But just for that moment, something about the lift of his chin, the angle of his head, had been Edward.

She had not told Kay. Edward had been killed in Arras in the spring of 1917; it did not seem an auspicious resemblance. Alice could remember quite clearly the moment when Lorna had come to tell her about the telegram. Lorna had not needed to say anything. Alice had known.

"Time to go to bed," she said to the purring cat. She knew she was being morbid and super-stitious, wallowing in her memories. Edward's death had been a terrible loss, but later there had been Patrick, and then Kay. Life reasserted itself, if you let it. She had been unlucky, but she had had five years of happiness, living in Dublin with Patrick, her lovely Patrick. And she still had Kay.

Realising that she had still made no move to get up and get ready for bed, she turned off the wireless and the reading lamp. She said, "Happy New Year," to the cat as she lifted her into the basket, and went through to her bed-room.

PART TWO:
1944—45

E-EASY

"*A* Shakespeare play? With all the interruptions we're bound to get?" Simon's voice echoed around the empty theatre. "You must be off your rocker, Charlie."

"Haven't you got enough to do on B Flight?" said Mac, a fitter from A Flight, who had been one of the chorus "girls" in the revue. "We could do with an extra pair of hands up our end. We don't sit about waiting for the NAAFI van and practising ruddy *Hamlet*."

"It isn't *Hamlet*," Charlie said, grinning. "It's *A Midsummer Night's Dream*."

"Oh yes," Simon said drily. "An obvious choice, I suppose, for the middle of winter."

"Don't ask me to be Queen of the ruddy Fairies," Mac said.

"I wasn't going to," Charlie said. "I thought you could be Puck."

Everyone looked at Mac. He was small and dark, and although he was about thirty he had a mischievous face and the grin of a naughty schoolboy.

"Typecasting," Mike said, improvising a few bars on the piano. "Seriously, though, Charlie, don't you think it's a bit much to take on?"

"We won't do all of it," Charlie said. "Just some of the scenes, with cuts. The good thing about it is the groupings of different characters. We can arrange the rehearsals around the shifts, and we won't need to have everyone at once."

There was a brief silence while Mike doodled abstractedly at the piano. We might as well all say yes and get on with it, Kay thought; once Charlie's set his mind on something, it's going to happen, whatever obstacles other people might point out.

"I think it's a good idea," Joyce said. "It'll be a challenge. And it'll make a change from another revue or pantomime. We've done enough of those."

"I thought you could be Helena," Charlie said. "You know, one of the lovers who gets mixed up. She's got to be tall and fair. And Kay, you could be Hermia."

"Hernia?" Mac said doubtfully. "Has she got to wear a truss or something?"

"Her*mia*," Charlie said. "With an m for mother. We'll have a bit of trouble finding Lysander and Demetrius, the handsome lovers. No problem with the rude mechanicals though."

"That sounds more like you and me, Charlie. We're mechanicals all right." Mac held out his hands, displaying oil-stained fingers and chipped nails. "And the rudeness bit won't be difficult."

"We'll cut out most of the fairy business," Charlie said. "I can't see too many volunteers rushing forward. We can make do with Oberon, Titania and Puck."

"Are you going to be in it yourself?" Kay asked, "or just direct the rest of us?"

"Just direct, she says," Charlie appealed to the group. "Anyone would think that was the easy bit, getting you lot into some sort of order. Well, I have got a part in mind, depending on who else turns up. I thought," he said, assuming a dignified expression. "I might play Bottom."

Kay began to look forward to it.

Missing David, she had time on her hands. One afternoon, muffled up against the bitter east wind, she walked round the perimeter of the airfield. By dispersals, teams of ground crew were swarming all over the Lancasters, checking and preparing them, like grooms tending racehorses. Or workers tending queen bees . . . that was a better comparison. The Lancasters were like queen bees: dozens of staff worked at servicing them, pampering them, getting them ready to fly. Everyone's work on the whole station, whether directly or indirectly, was geared towards sending the Lancasters to the enemy . . .

She emerged from her reverie to realise that someone was shouting at her.

"Oi! E-Easy to Kay! How do you receive me?"

It was Charlie Fox, in overalls, standing at the entrance door by E-Easy's tailplane.

"Strength niner," she shouted back.

"Fancy a look inside one of these contraptions?" he called. "Come on over and I'll show you round."

She walked underneath the vast spread of wing to the rear door. "Is it allowed?"

"Not really, but Flight's nowhere about."

She scrambled up the steps, and Charlie took her in. She was used to seeing the huge planes from the outside but the interior was surprisingly small, a narrow tunnel smelling of kerosene and polish. Small as she was, Kay had to stoop as they moved forward through the corridor of the fuselage towards the cockpit. Charlie helped her to climb over the bulky rear spar and main spar across the wings, and then sat her down in the pilot's seat. The cockpit was high above the ground in its Perspex dome; she could look along the port wing, where an engineer was perched on a ladder examining the inner engine, and back along to the mid-uppergunner's turret. Charlie showed her some of the pilot's instruments, and the throttle and the rudder bar, and the folding seat for the flight engineer. She imagined looking out from her position into black sky, at some unseen, unsuspecting German city. Or, more likely, it would be at the soaring fireworks of flak and tracer bullets, and the enemy searchlights . . . it felt horribly exposed.

"Five thousand horsepower, in those four engines," Charlie said proudly. He moved back to show her the navigation desk, lengthways against the side of the plane, with the seat facing an array of dials and indicators on the port side. "And this is where young Lochinvar sits. Or would, if this was his kite."

Kay did not mind Charlie teasing her about David, not any more. She looked at all the instruments whose workings David understood, the curtains to enclose the navigator in a blacked-out cubicle while he was working, and the elastic straps for holding compasses and pencils in place. She thought of David sitting there twenty thousand feet up, working away at his readings and bearings, filling in the log in his neat sloping handwriting. Concentrating hard, to keep his fear under control. Her stomach lurched at the thought of his vulnerability, up in the predatory sky above Germany, while the flak soared and the fighters swooped in for the kill like hyenas . . . It terrified her to think of it.

Charlie slapped his hand on a grey metal box with a round screen at the right-hand end of the desk. "And this box of tricks is the Gee-box. Clever blokes, navigators are. They have to be, to cope with this lot and still keep a calm head."

He showed her the other crew positions: the bomb aimer's, below and in front of the pilot's feet; the wireless op's, just behind the navigator, with an astrodome above; the mid-uppergunner's and the rear gunner's. Kay was amazed at how small the turrets were, pitying the poor gunners who had to sit cramped in them all the way to Germany and back. David had told her that of all aircrew jobs he would most hate to have the rear gunner's: completely isolated, with not much to do for most of the trip, unable to see where he was going, and plenty of time to work up a cold sweat.

Every surface and screen and handhold was immaculately clean, but Charlie fussed around with a cloth, giving an extra loving polish here and there. He made Kay think of a boarding house landlady taking round a prospective guest, showing how comfortable the rooms were.

"Tell you what," he said, "I'll arrange for you to go up in the old crate, if you like, on a flight test."

"What? Me, fly? How?"

Charlie tapped the side of his nose. "Leave it to me. Do you want to? I'll have a word with Mr Tait. He'll do it as a favour. But keep it under your hat."

Kay knew that it was strictly forbidden for WAAF to fly in operational aircraft, although one or two had been allowed to go on training flights, with special permission. But to go up in a Lancaster . . . it was a treat not to be missed, though she didn't know why Charlie thought Flying Officer Tait would agree. He was an amiable blond Scottish youth, a gangling six-footer only recently posted to Windersby. She had spoken to him once or twice in the Watch Office, but did not see why he would risk breaking the rules for her.

However, Charlie pulled strings, and two days later he told her to be ready outside the hangar. Charlie had provided her with a helmet and parachute, and the crew formed a group round her as they walked out to the aircraft. Kay's insides were churning and she was half wishing she hadn't accepted, but E-Easy's crew seemed to think it quite a joke to be concealing a stowaway. This flight test was just a routine for them, no more exciting than a bus ride.

Bombers had been circling the base all morning, as they always did before ops.

"Welcome aboard," Alistair Tait said, grinning at her from the pilot's seat as she scrambled forward. "Pleasure flights by special arrangement. It's probably best if you go and stand next to Digger." He indicated the navigator, a big Australian in the dark blue uniform of his country's air force.

"Just got to check my toys," the Australian told her cheerfully, "and then there'll be nothing for me to do. We're on visual, just a quick flip and down in time for lunch."

Alistair called each crew member in turn over the intercom, and then he and the flight engineer went through a series of checks. "Number two tanks on, Booster coil on, pulsometer pumps on, master cock on, ignition on, contact starboard inner . . ." and then Kay could hear no more above the revving of the four big Merlin engines and the vibration of the fuselage. There were a great many more checks before the plane was cleared to take off. Alistair taxied slowly round to the runway; there was an exhilarating surge of power and then E-Easy was racing forward at speed, bumping slightly on the runway. Kay felt the tail lift, and only a slight swaying told her that the plane was airborne. She tried not to feel sick, determined not to disgrace herself. To keep her mind off her queasy stomach, she thought of five thousand horses pulling the plane into the air, an enormous chariot team . . . The navigator was reading off airspeeds from his indicator, the flaps slid back into the wings, the nose dropped slightly and they were flying. Kay's stomach slowly righted itself. Out of the port side window she could see the horizon tilting and then levelling. Alistair's big hands moved calmly over the controls. The fields below were a dull patchwork of irregular shapes, all in winter colours, ploughed earth, turnip fields and pale grass, intersected by a road heading north, straight and direct as a ruled line on a map. Lincoln Cathedral came into view, proud above the cluster of red rooftops, as David had described it. She smiled as she imagined his surprise when she told him she had flown in a Lancaster. The navigator gave her a thumbs-up sign, and she realised that she was enjoying herself. The Lancaster banked round in a wide circle and soon she saw their own airfield, the big triangle of the runways and the aircraft dotted along the perimeter.

The navigator said something into his intercom and then listened while Alistair said something back. They were only about a yard apart, but the engine noise was so loud that they had to communicate over the intercom. When the conversation was over, the navigator beckoned to Kay and shouted at her, "I was just telling

Skip to get a move on. It's sausage and chips for lunch and if we're late we'll be stuck with leftovers."

They were descending, the runway swinging into view. The plane landed so smoothly that Kay did not feel it touch down. There was a final surge on the engines and then a silence which rang in her ears.

"E-Easy, Ground Flight to ground. Over."

Kay thanked Alistair Tait profusely and got down the steps on unsteady legs. The rest of the crew smuggled her back into the hangar.

"Come on ops next time you want to take to the air," the navigator said. "I'd rather have you to look at than old Loopy here."

The wireless operator he was referring to gave him a friendly shove as they went off for their lunch.

"What is it with you and navigators?" Charlie said, taking back the helmet and parachute.

"Thanks, Charlie, for arranging it. It was terrific."

"Anything to keep my star actors happy."

Going back to her billet, Kay passed one of the more officious WAAF Admin staff, Flight Sergeant Bellingham, known to Kay and Felicity as Bellyache. Kay tried to compose her face, picturing the pop-eyed, apoplectic reaction if Bellingham had the slightest idea what she had just been doing.

*　　*　　*

Felicity was envious when Kay told her about the secret flight. "But I'm glad to know that even you can break the rules sometimes. It does add a certain spice to life, does it not?'"

"I'm not planning to do it on a regular basis," Kay said.

Felicity sighed. "Even I'm not doing anything the Queen Bee could object to at the moment. More's the pity."

Her romance with Ian had ended abruptly when he had been posted to Bomber Command Headquarters at High Wycombe, and there seemed to be no plans for further meetings.

"I'm sure you'll think of something," Kay said.

"I don't know. I might apply for a posting myself."

"Why?" Kay asked, in dismay.

"I need a change of scene. I'm bored here."

Kay hoped she would change her mind. She did not want to lose Felicity. There had already been changes. Simon had gone on a training course, and Stephanie had been moved to the smaller satellite station; one of the flying control officers, Flight Lieutenant Smithers, had been posted to Scampton, and was replaced by Squadron Leader Roberts, not a popular substitute.

"You could always have a part in *A Midsummer Night's Dream*," Kay suggested.

"Charlie's always trying to rope new people in, especially now that he's lost Simon and one or two others."

"I might," Felicity said without enthusiasm. "But you know me. I can never stick at anything."

She seemed uncharacteristically listless, spending her off-duty time reading in their room. Kay wondered whether she had cared for Ian more than she had pretended; her usual attitude of *easy come, easy go* did not seem to be working.

David came back and joined his new crew. Kay thought it must have been rather odd for him, twice having been placed in established teams; most crews formed themselves before flying on ops and stayed together throughout their tours. She sensed that David did not hit it off with Sandy Beacham, although he said nothing about it. Beacham, an officer, did not mix much with the rest of the crew when not flying.

Kay's pleasure at having David back was mixed with her fear for him flying on operations. It was hard to readjust to the public life of Windersby, after the shift in their relationship over the Christmas and New Year leave. There was little opportunity for privacy, even when they managed to get off camp together. She hated to think that their time together could be the subject of gossip and speculation, although it was inevitable.

One night, lingering on the way back from the camp cinema, David whispered fiercely, "God, I wish . . ."

Just then a WAAF duty officer came along with a torch and said with apparent enjoyment, "Get along to your billets now."

David sighed and said abruptly, "Good night, Kay," and stomped off to his hut without telling her what he did wish.

Sometimes it frightened her, the way she felt when she was with him. She did not know what to do about it, only that she felt such a conflicting mixture of emotions that she could hardly call it happiness. Although they did not discuss it, she had the sense that they were both waiting for something, waiting for the proper time.

At the beginning of February, the moon period, all the crews were stood down and most were sent on leave. As David had only just had leave, he was kept on to help train a group of newly arrived navigators in the use of H2S radar for target-finding. It was the longest stand-down period Kay had known; only one or two minor operations took place, and then heavy falls of snow put paid to flying altogether. All available staff were put to work shovelling snow from the roads and runways, a strenuous but enjoyable task. With no operational flying, there was a lightening of the atmosphere, almost as if it were a holiday.

One evening David and some of the other remaining aircrew staged a snowball ambush as Kay and her colleagues finished their shift at the Watch Office. The victims mounted a vigorous counter-attack, and the fight was only briefly interrupted when Squadron Leader Roberts, on his way in, caught a snowball square in the chest of his greatcoat. Everyone had to stop and salute, Kay uncomfortably aware of ice trickling down inside her collar, while the squadron leader brushed himself down and glared.

"Really, must you behave like children?"

"Yes, we must," Kay muttered at his departing back view. No one else, she thought, would have objected to a bit of harmless off-duty fun; don't we deserve it?

By next morning, a very military snowman had appeared outside the Watch Office, complete with cap, moustache and salute.

Kay had hoped that the stand-down marked the end of the Berlin bombing. But as more new planes were delivered from the factories, and new crews arrived to fly them, it became apparent that the lull was not an ending, but merely an interval: a mustering of forces for an all-out effort.

The rest of David's crew returned from leave and operations started again on February 15th. The reprieve was over.

Rehearsal

*T*here had been a light ground mist when the Lancasters took off for an early evening raid. With the coming of darkness, it had quite suddenly thickened into a swirling fog, clamped over the airfield and deadening all sound.

"We're going to have to divert them further inland, surely, sir?" Mike said to Squadron Leader Roberts.

Kay waited beside the radio set. David was up there somewhere in K-King, and unless someone made a decision soon the sky would be filled with Lancasters circling in the gloom.

"Some of them will be short of fuel," Roberts said. He thought for a moment, while everyone waited. Then he said, "Tell Flight Lieutenant Beacham to try it. If he can do it, I'll get him in here to talk down the less experienced pilots."

Felicity, who for once was on the same watch as Kay, called K-King and told Sandy Beacham to land, giving him the airfield barometric pressure to set on his altimeter. Mike and Kay exchanged silent glances which said that the decision should have been taken sooner: it was rare for the whole country to be fog-bound, and while the aircraft still had fuel they could be diverted to a safer landing place. Roberts told Mike to contact Graveley with a warning, and from then on Kay was fully occupied in logging calls as the returning planes joined the circuit. She knew that Sandy Beacham would be landing virtually blind, a difficult task for the most experienced of pilots. Outside, the chance light was on as well as the glim-lamps, and the tower light was switched to green. The crash wagon and the fire tender went out past the window. Kay continued to log the conversations, watching her hand writing as if it belonged to someone else, amazed at her self-control, while her heart pounded against the buttons of her tunic so fiercely that she could almost hear it, and she hardly dared look up. It was all so horribly reminiscent of her first Darky call, with the crucial difference that this time she was not just a shocked onlooker but personally involved: up there, mentally, with David, sitting at his navigation desk with nothing to do but wait, having done his job of guiding the plane back to base. Now it was all up to the pilot.

Any comfort Kay may have been given by Sandy Beacham's being singled out as the most accomplished pilot was cancelled by her knowledge of what could happen if he didn't succeed. Her ear was sharply attuned to the descending throb of K-King's engines. However strictly she tried to keep her mind focused on her duties, she could not stop herself from seeing the Darky plane shooting out of the sky to crash in flames, beyond anyone's power to help. The fire tender waited, ominously.

"There she is," Mike exclaimed, and all eyes turned to K-King's navigation lights as she came down out of the fog. Her looming dark shape shot along the runway and passed out of sight. Too fast? No one spoke. And then, "K-King, Ground flight to ground," Sandy Beacham's voice said calmly over the loud-speaker. "It's a bit dicey, actually. I wouldn't recommend anyone else to try it."

Relief flooded like a soothing drug. K-King was safely down, and the crash wagon not needed.

"If Sandy says it's a bit dicey," Mike said, "that's roughly translated as absolutely lethal."

"Get on to Graveley," Roberts told him, and then said to the R/T operators, "Tell them to go on to Graveley. They'll have FIDO there to get them down. They'll see it from the air."

FIDO was Fog Investigation Dispersal Operation – an emergency system recently installed at some airfields: flare-filled trenches alongside a runway, to guide the planes in. There would be no more landings at Windersby that night. Felicity began to transmit the instructions, and Kay carried on filling in the log, wondering whether she would be able to see David when she came off duty.

No one liked being on shifts with Squadron Leader Roberts. He had joined the RAF before the war and regarded all wartime recruits as inefficient amateurs. He was only about forty, but his manner made him seem older; he had a clipped moustache and thin lips set in a permanently sour expression, as if nothing he saw pleased him. He was much stricter about discipline in the Watch Office than any of the other flying control officers.

In particular, since the snowball fight, he seemed to disapprove of Kay. When Charlie wanted to arrange an extra evening rehearsal for the whole cast, Kay asked Roberts if she could change shifts with Felicity. None of the other FCOs would have made any objection, as long as all the shifts were covered, but Roberts' face assumed an expression of distaste, as if Kay had suggested something improper.

"I don't know whether it occurs to you, Leary, when you're making arrangements for your social life, but we are trying to conduct a war. That seems to me rather more important than dressing up in fancy costumes and parading about on a stage. The shifts will stay exactly as listed."

On another occasion, Kay arrived early for her shift and realised that her period was starting earlier than expected. She had no choice but to race back across camp to get what she needed from her room and visit the bathroom. When she got back, Roberts was standing by the Control Bench looking pointedly at the clock.

"Five minutes late," he said stiffly.

"I'm sorry, I—"

"There's no excuse for being late on duty. None whatsoever. See that it doesn't happen again."

"Yes, sir," Kay said resentfully. She always made a point of arriving a few minutes early, rather than rushing in on the dot as Felicity sometimes did. It would have to be Squadron Leader Roberts who was on duty that day. Her usual reliability counted for nothing with him.

She poured out her grievances to Felicity that evening, annoyed at being found fault with for a second time.

"You should have told him why you came back. I would have done," Felicity said.

"But I couldn't say that, not to someone like him. Besides, he didn't give me much chance."

"I shouldn't let him get you down. Ignore him," Felicity said. She had washed and set her hair and was plucking her eyebrows, squinting into a hand-mirror.

"Going somewhere special?" Kay asked, pleased that Felicity had got over her depressed phase.

"Just out for dinner."

"Aha! Who with, this time?"

Felicity looked at her archly over the top of the mirror. "Well, actually, with Sandy."

"With the inscrutable Mr Beacham? My goodness, however did you mange that?"

"I didn't *manage* it, as you rather insultingly put it. It was his suggestion, surprisingly enough. He's very nice when you get to know him."

Kay found this difficult to believe. She had met Flight Lieutenant Beacham in the Control Office on several occasions, finding him one of the least approachable of the aircrew she had met. Perhaps Felicity regarded him as a challenge.

"Another officer, too," she remarked. "You've definitely promoted yourself from the ranks, then?"

"One comes to expect a certain style,"

Felicity said, in her self-mocking way. "There, that'll have to do."

Kay looked round at the uninviting room and decided that it was too cold to stay, especially if Felicity was going out. "It's freezing in here. I'm going to the NAAFI to warm up." On her way out she thought of something and poked her head back round the door. "Perhaps you could get your irresistible charm to work on Squadron Leader Roberts, and see if you can make him a little bit more human?"

Felicity grimaced. "Now there I do draw the line."

Dear Kay, Alice wrote from home, *I'm afraid I have just heard that there is bad news about Stephen. He was reported "Missing, Believed Killed" when flying on operations a week ago. Jack wrote to tell me. Of course he is absolutely distraught, and coming so soon after Stephen's marriage it is particularly tragic. I know how upset you will be as you were so fond of Stephen. The only crumb of comfort is that it isn't definite . . ."*

Kay closed her eyes and leaned her head against the wall behind her bed. She had saved the letter as a treat for when she came off duty . . . Only a fortnight ago she had received a letter from Uncle Jack enclosing a photograph of Stephen's wedding in Dublin. Poor

Mary . . . Stephen must have barely returned from his brief honeymoon leave. The photograph stood on her bedside locker: Stephen, immaculate in uniform with the pilot's wings he had always wanted, his attractive young bride smiling up at him, Uncle Jack and Aunt Sarah looking on proudly. Whenever Kay thought of Stephen, she pictured him on horseback; he was a wonderful rider, like Uncle Jack, able to cope with the most difficult horses. It seemed to be a natural gift with both of them. They spoke Horse, as she thought of it; they didn't need to use spurs or harsh bits to make horses do what they wanted. She always imagined that Stephen would fly a plane in the same effortless way, coaxing it, making it want to please him. He needn't have volunteered; he could have stayed in Ireland. Kay could imagine how Uncle Jack and Aunt Sarah must be feeling. They hadn't wanted him to go.

She wrote to them that evening, knowing how useless sympathy must be. "Missing Believed Killed", offered a crumb of comfort, her mother had said, but Kay thought that perhaps "Killed In Action" would almost be preferable; at least then you'd *know*.

She said nothing to anyone about the news, not even to David. It was a private loss she would have to come back to, when there was time to take it in properly. Tragic as it was for her family, Stephen's loss was just one among hundreds at this time of intensive bombing effort.

Morale seemed low among the aircrew at present. How could it be otherwise, when so any planes failed to return? The winter weather did not favour long flights over Germany and yet big operations were being mounted night after night. Four different aircraft carried the name Q-Queen within ten days; three crews went missing, twenty-one men. Each new aircraft to bear that code letter seemed doomed. When an experienced crew was told to fly the new Q-Queen they refused to go near it; eventually the latest one survived a raid and the taboo passed. Kay wondered whether the losses could be justified. Whatever damage the raids were doing to enemy production, could it really be set against this endless throwing away of lives, like columns drawn up on some callous account sheet? She was thankful that David flew with an experienced pilot and not with one of the new crews who came and went before anyone learned to recognise their faces. If anyone could survive, it would be Sandy Beacham. Kay did not know how the aircrews stood the strain – risking their lives at night, coming back for interrogation and a few hours' sleep, flight testing, snatching a nap in the afternoon, then often briefing again for ops that same night. They were well-fed, with extras which the other camp personnel did not get: sugar, cream, eggs and bacon. It seemed horribly like fattening them up for the kill.

One morning Kay arrived on duty to see burnt fragments being cleared up from the airfield, the ground scarred by impact. Two Lancasters had collided over Windersby on their return, with the loss of both crews. Kay had known one of the pilots as a slight acquaintance and had spoken to him only the day before as he went in to briefing. The brutal suddenness of it horrified her. Life seemed such a fragile thing, vulnerable to the whims of chance or fate or human fallibility.

David no longer said much about flying, but one thing he did tell Kay was that he could never get used to the sudden transitions; within a few hours of being in the bomber stream over the Ruhr, he could be joking with friends in the Mess bar. And vice versa.

Rehearsals were progressing, in spite of various crises and cast changes, but Kay's heart was not in it. She shouldn't have come tonight; she was no use to Charlie and the others. Charlie had had to scour the camp and do a good bit of arm-twisting before he had filled the roles of Lysander and Demetrius. Larry, the armourer who had been cast as Lysander, was a cheerful and willing boy whose blond good looks suited the part, although he was completely wooden as an actor. They were working on the scene in which he was to desert Hermia/Kay for Helena/Joyce.

"Look," Charlie said with enormous patience, "you're word-perfect on your lines – which is more than can be said for anyone else – but you're supposed to be trying to get away from Hermia. Sneer. That's better," he said encouragingly as Larry arranged his features into an unconvincing scowl. "Now say the *vile thing, let loose* bit. Kay, hang on to his arm. Larry, shake her off – pretend she's a disgusting leech or something . . ."

They performed the scene lethargically. Charlie gave Kay an odd look.

"Come on, Kay, put some effort into it, for Pete's sake. You did it ten times better last time. What's the matter with you tonight?"

"Oh, nothing," she mumbled. "Let's do it again then, Larry."

She made an effort to cheer up, for Charlie. Perhaps it would have been better to drop out of the play, but she knew she would miss it; the sociability of rehearsals usually helped her to forget her worries. Poor Charlie – she wasn't being fair to him at all, after all the effort he made to hold things together. Without him, there would be no plays or revues at all; no one else had his determination.

They did the scene twice more, Kay trying to match Joyce's brisk professionalism. At last some progress was made, and Charlie said, "All right, we'll call it a day. Thanks, everyone. Keep practising the sneer, Larry."

"I'm going over to the NAAFI before it closes," Joyce said, looking at her watch. "Coming, Kay?"

"No, I don't think so, thanks," Kay said. She went into the small dressing room backstage to collect her coat. When she came back, the others had gone, and David had come in and was talking to Charlie. Relief warmed her at the sight of him, even though she had checked that K-King was safely down from the late afternoon minelaying raid before she had come to the rehearsal. David, still in battledress and flying jacket, must have come straight from debriefing and the post-flight meal. It was wet and windy outside, and his hair glistened with rain. He looked tired and drawn.

Charlie was jingling a bunch of keys in his hand, but he stopped and looked from Kay to David and back again. Kay guessed that he thought they had had an argument, in view of her downcast mood earlier and David's subdued manner now.

"Ah,' he said. "Er . . . I'll leave you two to

lock up, shall I? The keys go back to the Orderly Room. Only be careful – the Queen Bee comes round at ten."

He gave Kay the keys and slipped out through the blackout trap. David and Kay looked at each other. They had the place to themselves for half an hour. David took the keys and went to the door and locked it from the inside, and then he and Kay went through to the dressing room, where there was a shabby velvet sofa sometimes used as a stage prop. David sat down and pulled her against him, but did not say anything. He seemed so tired that she wondered why he hadn't gone straight to bed.

"How was it?" she said, thinking that perhaps something awful had happened on the raid.

"It was all right. Sandy Beacham went on compassionate leave as soon as we got back. His father's seriously ill. There was a message for him."

"Oh."

"So now we haven't got a pilot."

"Perhaps you'll be stood down tomorrow, then."

"Perhaps," David said, as if that hardly mattered. "I haven't had much of a wash yet. I probably smell awful."

She sniffed. "Rum, mostly."

"From debriefing. To send us to sleep, not that I'll need any help. But I wanted to talk to you first."

"What about?"

But for several minutes they did not talk at all. The half hour of privacy was an unusual bonus, with no prowling admin staff to chivvy them apart. The admin WAAFs knew exactly where to go to flush out courting couples; Kay resented them for making it seem sordid. She tried to remember to keep one ear open for the duty officer on her rounds, but could keep no grip on common sense while David was holding her close, caressing her and looking at her in that peculiarly intense way that made her feel not quite in control . . .

It was David who pulled away first. "Kay. Listen."

"Mmm?"

He pushed a loose strand of hair back from her face. "How would you feel about getting married? We could, if you'd like to."

She stared at him. "You want to marry me? Is that a proposal?"

"I suppose so. Yes, it is. I'll get down on one knee and do it properly, if you like. But please say yes."

She leaned back against him, gazing at a clutter of stage swords and moth-eaten wigs in a corner of the room where she and Charlie had put them after the sorting. She could feel his heart beating.

"When?" she said.

His mouth brushed her ear and the side of her neck. "Is that *Yes*?"

"No, wait – how soon do you mean?"

"Well, soon. What's the matter?" He caught hold of her chin and turned her face towards his. "Don't you think it's a good idea?"

"Perhaps, I mean one day, yes, after the war, but not now." She saw the abrupt disappointment in his face. "We're too young."

"After the war," he repeated slowly, as if trying out the idea. "Who knows how long that might be? We might wait for years. You're eighteen, and I'm twenty-one, old enough to know that I love you and I want to marry you. I – well, I thought you felt the same."

"I do! But marriage – we've never talked about it . . ."

"We can talk about it now, can't we?"

"What would happen to us? We wouldn't be allowed to be on the same station and we'd see less of each other than we do now."

"But when I'm on leave we could be properly together, no need for hiding in corners like this, as if we're doing something wrong . . . we could get a place of our own, rent rooms or something."

"I might be posted to the north of Scotland or Cornwall or . . ."

"Don't keep making difficulties," he said

gently. "You could leave the WAAF, if you wanted to, if we were married."

Kay pictured herself in a cosy flat, decorative and feminine in civvies, a model wife, cooking delicious dinners for David and going to bed with him afterwards, instead of returning chastely to their bedsteads and biscuits. It appealed strongly, but reality intruded. I'd have to work in munitions or be a filing clerk, she thought. She saw herself working nine to five in some dreary office, coming home to an empty flat and waiting for news of David when he was on ops: not even knowing what was going on, just waiting, a service wife.

"But I don't want to leave the WAAF," she said.

David turned slightly away from her. "Don't you love me enough to want to marry me? I thought you'd be pleased."

"I am pleased, of course I . . ." she tried to explain. "It's a sort of superstitiousness, a feeling that if we did get engaged or married, then . . . well, something would happen."

Like whatever happened to Stephen. She had still not told David about it, and did not want to tell him now, not while he was flying on operations himself.

"I see," David said, rebuffed. "You don't want to be a widow, at your age. That's reasonable enough."

171

It was all going wrong, their precious time together spoiled by misunderstanding. "No, listen . . . it's not as . . . as calculating as you make it sound – it's not like that at all!" she protested. "If anything did happen, it couldn't make it any easier, or any worse, being married . . ."

"Then why won't you say yes, if it makes no difference?"

"Because . . . of all the things I've said."

He looked down, resigned. "I won't keep trying to persuade you. You seem to have made your mind up."

She could not bear to see him despondent. She traced a finger along his eyebrow. "I haven't! I *will* marry you, after the war, if you still want to."

His eyes searched her face. "But you don't even want an engagement, not now?"

"No . . . I don't want other people to know. We could think of ourselves as engaged, without telling anyone. Oh, David, don't look at me like that!"

She knew that she had hurt him, but could not think what to say to make him feel better. She could not rid herself of the superstitious fear – a foolish one, since what possible difference could it make? – that to formalise their relationship would be to offer David as a hostage to fortune. But she could not explain. It was cold and draughty in the dressing room, and soon they locked up and returned the key and went back through the rain to their separate quarters.

ON A CHARGE

When Kay came off duty at lunch time next day, she found Felicity packing her case.

"I didn't know you had a leave pass," she remarked. "You'd better hurry up if you want to get off camp before they close us off. There's ops tonight – they've been flight-testing all morning. Are you going home?"

"Good God, no. I'm going to London on a forty-eight-hour, to meet Sandy," Felicity said.

"But I thought he was on compassionate leave?"

"He is, but he can't be compassionate for twenty-four hours a day. I'm going to meet him at the Café Royal and we're going to stay in town overnight if he can book a room."

"You mean—'

Felicity turned and saw her expression and

said, "Yes, I mean— You should see your face! You're such an innocent, Kay. Don't be so prudish! I thought going out with David would have made you a bit more broad-minded."

"I'm not prudish," Kay said, although she thought that perhaps she was, at least about such casualness. "I'm just – well, surprised."

"I can't think why. It's not the first time, you know." Felicity was packing her evening dress, laying stockings along the folds of tulle so that it would not crease.

"But I didn't know you and Sandy were – are you in love with him?"

"Oh, Kay, don't ask such things." Felicity stooped to pick up a dropped stocking.

"Why not? It's relevant, isn't it?"

"We're not like you and David, if that's what you mean," Felicity said shortly.

Kay lapsed into a resentful silence. She was not sure what Felicity was implying by that, and did not understand how she could be so blasé about her relationship with Sandy. Sometimes it amazed her that she and Felicity could get on as well as they usually did, when they had so little in common. What would Felicity have thought of her conversation with David about marriage? She would probably think them both absurdly old-fashioned. Kay sat down on her bed, annoyed with Felicity but too tired to pursue the conversation. She kept thinking about David's wounded expression, wondering whether she could have explained her doubts more adequately. Apart from her conviction that they really were too young to marry, she could not help likening her situation to her mother's, in the last war. Alice had been engaged to Edward, her first love; they had arranged the date for their wedding, and then Edward had been killed near Arras, in the assault on Vimy Ridge. Alice had told Kay that afterwards it had seemed inevitable, a cruel reprisal for daring to throw down a gauntlet to fate. Kay had not told David about that, feeling that it would be unlucky to mention it. And then there was Stephen, shot down a few days after his wedding. She slumped uncomfortably on her bed and stared bleakly at the wall.

"Cheer up, it's not the end of the world. What's the matter? Has Roberts been coming the old acid again?" The air force slang sounded odd on Felicity's lips.

"No."

"What, then? You haven't argued with David, have you?"

"No, not really."

"At least he won't be on ops for a couple of days, with Sandy away."

"No. That's some consolation."

"Consolation for what?"

"Well, for . . . everything."

Felicity snapped her case shut. "Aren't you going in for lunch?"

"In a minute." Having let herself sit down, Kay felt too sluggish to get up again. She would be on duty again at midnight, and she needed sleep more than she needed her lunch. She said, "Do you think the war will end?"

Felicity laughed, dumping the case on the floor. "What a question! I suppose it must. How soon is anyone's guess."

"One year, five years . . . ten years?"

"God only knows." Felicity shrugged. "I suppose we'll slog it out. At least there are some hopeful things going on. The talk of a second front, for one. A landing in France."

"That's only a rumour," Kay said. "People were talking about that two years ago."

"Something's got to happen. At least the Germans are on the defensive now."

But was victory any nearer? Perhaps David was right, Kay thought, and they'd carry on as they were, doing their bit for the war until they were middle-aged. It was hard to imagine any other kind of life. But she felt too tired to think about it any more.

"Come on," Felicity said bracingly. "Food. You can sleep later."

Kay bumped into David by chance as she was leaving the cookhouse. He was going in for lunch with the rest of his crew, but he asked if she would meet him later, before his briefing.

"Briefing? But I thought you were stood down today, with no pilot?"

"So did we, but we're up there on the battle order as reserve crew, and it looks like we'll be going if they can't get J-Jig sorted out. Jig's pilot will fly with us."

They arranged to meet each other on the perimeter track in forty-five minutes' time. It's not fair, Kay told herself bitterly; the peace of mind she had promised herself for the next two or three days had been abruptly snatched away . . . She would never be able to get used to it, the thud of fear in her stomach when she knew David was on ops, no matter how easy the target. At least she would have the chance to put things right between them before he went.

"Have you any idea where it is tonight?" she asked him, as they walked along the edge of the airfield.

"Not yet – but look."

WAAF drivers had brought the tractors and bomb trains out to the waiting Lancasters, whose bomb doors open along the length of their bellies made them look like filleted fish. Armourers were carefully winching the bombs up into position. Bombs came in various shapes and sizes, and Kay could recognise the 4,000-lb high capacity bombs, big and clumsy as metal dustbins. And there were racks and racks of smaller ones, slimmer and more streamlined.

"Incendiaries," David said. "It's a town."

He did not need to tell her that it was likely to be Berlin, or how he felt about it.

"Perhaps J-Jig will be ready in time," she said.

David nodded towards a distant Lancaster. "She's over there, with her bomb doors closed. She won't be going."

"Wouldn't it be simpler to transfer the whole crew together to your plane?"

"I suppose it would. But ours not to reason why."

They walked on without discussing it further.

"Where shall we go?" Kay said.

David looked at his watch. "There isn't long. Let's go through the gap in the fence, and get off camp, even if it's only for half an hour."

The gap in the six-foot perimeter fence, ineffectively bridged with barbed wire, was used by camp staff taking an unofficial short cut to the village pub. No one was watching. David climbed over the wire and held it down so that Kay would not catch her skirt on the barbs.

A path led diagonally across the potato field beyond, worn by many feet tramping back and forth to the Hare and Hounds, but David and Kay walked along the field boundary and out into a sheep meadow. It was a blowy March day, with a hint of warmth in the intervals between gusts: a day when winter and spring seemed to be competing for dominance, with spring winning. A skylark was singing overhead, and the hedgerows were misted green with the first delicate hawthorn leaves. David looked up at the thin streaks of cloud in a watercolour-washed sky. It was no good thinking you could get away from flying by leaving the airfield: Kay knew he was assessing the wind speed, and wondering how much cloud there would be over the target.

"When I saw you last night," he said, "I didn't tell you that Squadron Leader Wilson is recommending me for a commission."

"Is he? So you're going to be an officer? Do you have to apply for it?"

"Just a bit of form-filling, I think, but it'll be straightforward enough with his backing. It's not unusual."

"So you'll be Pilot Officer Evans? Or Flying Officer?" A thought struck her. "But we won't be able to see each other!"

"Of course we will! It doesn't stop Felicity, does it?"

"But not like we do now. Not like this. You won't even be able to go to dances in the Sergeants' Mess. You'll have to go and drink sherry with the wing commander and talk about cricket and fox-hunting."

"Good grief, Kay, this isn't the fourteen–eighteen war! Things have moved on a bit. And honestly," David said, more seriously, "I don't think it'll make that much difference. I was pleased when he told me. My first thought was that it'd be easier to get married on an officer's pay. But that was before you said you didn't want to get married."

"You know I didn't put it like that – I just said not *yet*. Oh, David, please don't let's argue." She took his hand, and his fingers curled round hers and he pulled her close enough to put his other arm round her.

"I'm not arguing. And there is one obvious answer, if you're worried about us not being able to see each other. Why don't you put in for a commission as well?"

"But I don't want one."

"That's silly. You'd get it, easily – you've got brains, you could pass the tests with no trouble."

"But what tests? I don't want to be an admin WAAF – they're the least popular people on the whole camp," Kay objected. "And if I apply for another trade I'll be posted away from here. I really don't want it. I'm happy as I am."

David released his arm from her shoulders and moved away from her. "I don't know what's the matter with you, Kay. Whenever I suggest anything you can only see problems. I

181

suppose it's understandable that you don't want to get married, but you don't seem to want to improve your own position and you haven't even said you're pleased about my chance of a commission. I really don't understand you."

They glared at each other.

"No," she said. "Perhaps you don't."

His eyes met hers with an expression of hurt bafflement. She regretted the words as soon as she had said them, but they were there, indelible, as if written in the air in giant capital letters.

"Well, then," David said quietly, "there doesn't seem any point in talking about it any more, does there? We may as well go back. I mustn't be late for briefing."

He turned and walked away fast along the hedgerow, head down, his shoulders set in an unapproachable hunch. Kay stumbled after him in dismay.

"David, wait! Come back! I'm sorry – I don't know why I said it . . . please . . ."

But he would not stop, even when she ran up to him and pulled at his arm. She was nearly in tears of frustration and self-reproach – how could she have said something so unkind to David, whom she loved, and who might have to fly to Berlin that same night?

"*Please* listen—"

And then he did stop, but he was looking ahead, at the gap in the wire. Someone was there, looking out across the field at them. David swore softly.

"Come over here at once," a man's voice shouted.

They crossed the potato field. The man who had summoned them was a stout corporal with the sleeve chevrons denoting Service Police. Kay knew that it was too late to disguise their intentions: they had obviously broken out of camp, and were intending to break back in.

The corporal gestured to them to get back over the barbed wire. "What were you doing out there?"

"Talking," David said, with an edge of insolence.

"How did you leave the camp?"

"Through the gap," David said. There was no point in denying it, since the corporal would be certain to check at the main gate and find that they hadn't booked out.

"Show me your 1250s," the corporal said.

They got out their identity cards and he wrote down their names and numbers in a notebook.

"You're on a charge," the corporal snapped. "Both of you. Report to the guard room at sixteen-thirty. Is that clear?

"Yes, Corporal," Kay said.

"Is that clear?" the man repeated to David.

"Yes, thank you," David said coolly, although Kay knew he had no intention of going, since he would be at briefing.

Kay tried to catch his eye, but he walked off along the perimeter track without another glance at her.

"Escort, accused and witness, qui-ick march!" barked Flight Sergeant Bellingham.

Kay wished Bellyache didn't have to give the impression of enjoying the proceedings. She was the kind of WAAF admin officer whose idea of discipline was to imagine everything her subordinates might enjoy doing, and to find reasons why they should not be allowed to do it.

"Le-eft, wheel. Halt!" Bellingham stamped to attention in front of the section officer's desk and saluted smartly.

"Escort, accused and witness all present, ma'am."

Kay stood to attention between the SP corporal and the escort, an Admin Office clerk, facing the section officer's desk. It was ridiculous, the formality – anyone might think she was accused of high treason instead of simply slipping out of camp. She supposed that David would have to go through the same procedure next day. She hoped that being on a charge would not jeopardise his chances of a commission.

Section Officer Cummings, the "Queen Bee", a woman of about forty, sat at her desk looking mildly at Kay, as if she too found the procedure tedious.

"Thank you, Flight. You may stand escort and witness at ease."

"Escort and witness, stand at . . . ease!"

Kay stamped her feet apart and held her hands loosely together behind her back. Mrs Cummings picked up the charge sheet.

"Are you 579127 ACW Leary, K.?"

"Yes, ma'am."

"579127 Leary, K., you are charged that While on Active Service Contrary to King's Regulations Clause, Air Force Law and Station Standing Orders, paragraph 5, you did fail to book out of the station. Two. Further that you did break into the site. Do you plead guilty or not guilty?"

"Guilty to the first part, ma'am. The SP corporal told us to break back in."

"You were intending to break back in, though, presumably?"

"Yes, ma'am."

Mrs Cummings asked the SP corporal for his report.

"I observed the accused and an airman later identified as Flight Sergeant Evans in a field beyond the perimeter fence. When I questioned them they admitted that they had broken out of

185

camp through a gap in the fence and were about to re-enter by the same route."

"Thank you." Mrs Cummings turned to Kay. "Why did you and Flight Sergeant Evans find it necessary to break out of camp?"

Kay hesitated. "We wanted to talk in private. We were having an argument, ma'am."

"I see." Mrs Cummings' eyes rested on Kay's face with a hint of amusement. "I hope it was satisfactorily concluded?"

"No, ma'am, it wasn't."

Mrs Cummings said, more severely, "You do understand how important it is that security is kept before operations? That, in fact, you left the camp at a time when leaving was strictly forbidden?"

"Yes, ma'am."

"Did you or Flight Sergeant Evans speak to anyone else while you were off the premises?"

"No, ma'am. We didn't see anyone."

Mrs Cummings looked at the charge sheet again. "I find you guilty as charged. Do you wish to be tried by court martial? Or will you accept my punishment?"

Good grief! A court martial, for ten minutes off camp? They'd be lining up the firing squad next. Didn't the admin staff have anything better to do? And if they had any idea what Felicity was planning to do, this very night, her own misdemeanour would fade into insignificance . . .

"Your punishment, ma'am."

"Your behaviour was irresponsible and quite inexcusable. Not something I would have expected of you."

"Yes, ma'am." Kay kept her eyes fixed on the wall just behind Section Officer Cummings' head.

"You have a good record otherwise, apart from one instance of lateness on duty. Take good care that you don't appear before me again for such a foolish reason. I sentence you to three days Confined to Camp, with extra duties."

Bellingham and the SP corporal stared ahead, faces expressionless. Kay guessed that they both thought her punishment too light.

"And for future reference, Leary," Mrs Cummings concluded, "should you and Flight Sergeant Evans wish to pursue your contretemps, I think you'll find there are plenty of suitable venues within the confines of the station."

TARGET BERLIN

*K*ay had given up all idea of getting any sleep before going on shift. In her room she had stored some caffeine tablets, the "wakey-wakey" pills supplied to aircrew for night ops, which David had given her on a previous occasion when she had feared falling asleep on duty. But she did not think she would fall asleep tonight.

David's afternoon and early evening would be taken up with navigators' briefing, main briefing, the pre-flight meal, and then kitting up and collecting equipment from the crew rooms and parachute section. After that, a lorry took all the crews round to their aircraft, now stationed at the various pans round the field. There would always be a gathering of ground staff to see them off. When she heard the lorries driving out along the perimeter, Kay put on her greatcoat and followed them along the row of dim blue lights which marked the edge of the track. She did not know whether David would speak to her, but she had to do something.

She turned her collar up against the cold north wind. There seemed to be some hold-up. Crews were waiting impatiently, some stamping their booted feet, some sitting down on the grass to wait, smoking. They wore a variety of flying gear to protect them from the cold at high altitudes, and the rear gunners could be distinguished by the bulky electrical suits designed to stop them from freezing in their turrets. The group captain was being driven round in a jeep to each plane in turn, talking to the pilots. Kay thought she would be sent back if he saw her approaching the crews, but she knew where K-King had been standing earlier and she made her way directly to it. Then she saw Isaacs, the bomb aimer from David's crew, standing by himself smoking a cigarette. She called to him and asked him to get David to come over. She thought it likely that David would refuse, but she heard Isaacs say, "Evans, your girlfriend's come to see you off," and saw him point, and David came over to her in the half darkness. He was wearing a Sidcot flying suit, harness and helmet, and he carried his parachute in its canvas cover and the green bag which contained his navigation equipment.

"We're just about to get on board." He seemed on edge, and she knew that his head was probably full of co-ordinates and outward legs and turning points.

"I know. I wanted to see you. I'm sorry."

"It's all right." He looked at her and his expression softened. "Don't worry. I'll see you tomorrow."

"Good luck."

"It's all right," he said again. He transferred everything he was carrying to one arm and fished in a pocket of his flying suit with his free hand, and held out the little black china cat she had given him at Christmas. "Look. He always comes along."

She smiled, clasping the cat and his hand with it. His fingers tightened over hers, and he said, "What did you get from the chief WAAF?"

"Three days confined to camp."

"I'm sorry. That was my fault."

"Oh, David, that's the last thing I'm worried about . . . Is it Berlin?"

They both knew that she should not have asked and that he should not tell her – even the ground crews were not supposed to know the target. But his hesitation and fractional nod told her that it was. She would know anyway, as soon as she went on duty.

"Come on, Taff," a voice shouted. "It's no

use hoping we'll go without you. The old kite doesn't know the way."

David put the china cat back in his pocket. He leaned forward and kissed Kay quickly, and then turned and walked back to K-King.

The trolley-acc generator was plugged in ready to start the first engine. David climbed up the steps and disappeared through the rear door. Kay suddenly wanted to ask him whether the rest of the crew usually called him Taff, or Boyo, or just Evans. She felt momentarily jealous of the crew, because they knew David in a way she did not, in the enforced intimacy of airmen whose lives depended on each other's skill and quick reactions. Even Sandy Beacham, whom David did not much like, knew him in that way better than she did. She wanted to know how they talked to each other, what they said on those long flights to the target, and in the tense dangerous moments over it. She had forgotten to ask him about the pilot, who he was, and how experienced; she didn't even know his name. Somewhere behind her, out in the fields, she heard a screech owl; the eerie cry sent a shiver down her spine. The booster pump started up, followed by the slow turning over of the first engine and then its surge into life; then she saw the propellers of the next engine whirring, and then the other two. Soon the whole airfield was full of the noise of nearly twenty aircraft, cuffing and numbing the ears of the listeners. When the tests were completed, the pilot signalled to the ground crew to remove the chocks, and put his window up. Kay waved, in case David could see her, and went across to the runway to wait with the others who had gathered there. There was always a chance that the raid might be scrubbed, even at this stage. But soon the planes started to move slowly along the perimeter track, dragging their heavy tails. The first to go, E-Easy, flashed its code letter to Control, and the green light from the tower indicated clearance to take off. Kay had watched this procedure many times from the Flying Control bench, less frequently from the ground. In the office there was little to do at this stage but log the take-off times; radio silence was always observed during take-off and the early stages of a raid to avoid alerting the enemy. E-Easy thundered along the runway, the tail came up, balanced and poised, and then the plane lifted and climbed, blasting the watchers with its din. Next O-Orange, quickly airborne; now it was K-King, rushing past the waving spectators and taking off smoothly. Kay kept her eyes fixed on the navigation lights rising into the darkness until she was no longer sure she could distinguish them from the others. She could not let herself think about the deadly bomb-load carried in the plane's belly and what it might do to Berlin: she could only think about David.

The clamour of Merlin engines became a distant drone and then faded away. Silence settled over the airfield like an autumn fog, and the spectators gradually drifted away to their beds or their shifts or the NAAFI canteen.

Berlin. It would be a long wait.

Pilot Officer Coltwell was the name on the board opposite K-King. Kay had seen the name chalked up before but could put no face to it.

"Do you know who he is?" she asked Mike as they settled down for the long midnight-to-eight watch.

"Yorkshire lad – the tall one with long hair. Know who I mean?" Mike said. "He was at London University until he joined up. Plays a good game of soccer. Eleven ops flown, I think, and he's done the Berlin run three or four times. No problems that I know of."

A twelfth trip. Kay did not usually regard herself as superstitious, but at times like this she could not help it: she was glad it wasn't a thirteenth.

"At least they're not flying with a spare bod straight from O.T.U., then," she said.

"Pity about Sandy Beacham being off. This would have been last but one of his second tour. The rest of the crew will only have one more to do after this, except your David. I bet Sandy would have wanted to be with them."

Kay did not reply, knowing that Sandy Beacham, at this precise moment, was probably in bed with Felicity. Her attitude to his so-called compassionate leave was rather different now from when she had expected it to relieve David of flying. She tried to console herself by thinking of tonight's raid as one more to cross off from David's first tour.

They would not hear anything for at least an hour. Take-off had been soon after seven, and the flight to Berlin and back took six or seven hours. Kay was relieved that Squadron Leader Roberts was not on duty tonight as Flying Control Officer; instead it was Flight Lieutenant Armstrong, who simply got on with his work and let the staff get on with theirs, instead of hovering over their shoulders waiting for them to do something he could complain about. Alongside Kay and Mike on the control bench sat Jimmy, the young corporal, and a new WAAF, a shy girl called Helen; both these two made Kay feel like an old hand. After a while, Helen went off to make cocoa for everyone. Kay gazed out at the clear sky and remembered counting the stars in Pleiades with David. She had sat here through so many dusks and nights and dawns now that she felt she knew the sky and the airfield intimately, with the weather in all its moods. Conditions tonight were not the most benign: the wind had risen, and she could hear it moaning and wailing in the wires to the tower.

The loudspeaker crackling into life was a welcome intrusion into the room. The first bomber to return, C-Charlie, was crossing the coast, and within minutes was close enough for Kay to switch to local frequency.

"Venture C-Charlie calling Blackrock. Permission to land."

"Hello, C-Charlie, this is Blackrock, receiving you strength niner. Clear to land . . . call when on downwind leg."

C-Charlie touched down smoothly and taxied back to dispersals. Mike chalked the landing time on the board and phoned through to the Operations Room, and the crew went off for debriefing. It was half-past one. Nothing else happened for a long fifteen minutes. Then came the Scottish accent of Alistair Tait in E-Easy, followed by W-Willie and F-Fox. There were still fifteen more to come in. With the drone of each approaching engine Kay strained her ears for the voice which would announce the arrival of K-King. A-Able called down, and then U-Uncle . . .

There was still nothing from Pilot Officer Coltwell when one of the pilots came up to the Control Office to wait for friends. Kay could hear him talking to Flight Lieutenant Armstrong behind the blackout curtain, Armstrong's Oxford English and the pilot's New Zealand drawl.

"The Met people got it wrong. The wind out there was pushing us south the whole time, way off course. We got scattered all over the place. We hardly saw another kite on the way back . . ."

Their voices dropped, and Kay could only pick out snatches: ". . . bloody shambles. Night fighters must have picked us up on radar . . . markers drifting south . . . lost contact . . . they'll probably come straggling in in ones and twos."

They did. I-Item, with half her tail section shot away, and O-Orange. S-Sugar, calling for emergency services for her rear gunner. Z-Zebra, on three engines, overshooting the runway and having to make a second attempt. Gradually the gaps on the board were filled in. Mike, knowing of Kay's anxiety, kept trying to reassure her: "If they've been blown about, then they're just taking a longer route to get back. There's time yet. They'll be back, you'll see."

His intentions were kind but his words were meaningless to Kay. It was no good pretending that crews always did come back. Time was running out, as they all knew: the fuel would

196

not last indefinitely. Nothing had been heard from K-King's wireless operator, no ditching signal or request for new bearings or emergency instructions. The station commander, who had been waiting for the last three planes, shook his head and went away again. Kay stared numbly at her log book. Mike made her a cup of tea, which nearly choked her; Helen kept gazing at her in silent sympathy. Flight Lieutenant Armstrong rang the Operations Room and Intelligence, and found out that Alistair Tait's crew had seen a plane go down over the target, but were almost certain that it had had a different squadron marking. None of the returning crews had reported seeing anything of the missing three planes. When Kay's shift ended at eight a.m. there were still three blank spaces on the board, and one of them was against K-King.

EFFECTS

*T*he team for the next shift arrived, but Kay would not leave the Flying Control Office. Eventually, Mike convinced her that there was no point in waiting any longer, and made her go with him and Helen to the cookhouse for breakfast. She sat clutching her mug of tea, unable to eat anything. She had not slept for over twenty-four hours and was bleary-eyed with worry and exhaustion, her brain running in tired loops like a circuitry diagram, getting nowhere, returning always to the bald fact that K-King was not coming back.

Alistair Tait's flight engineer, a slight acquaintance since Kay's illicit flight, came over and said, "I'm sorry about David, Kay."

She could not answer, only stare dumbly at the table; he had made it sound so final.

"But no one *knows*," she said to Mike and Helen when he had gone; "no one *saw*. Anything could have happened. They could have bailed out, or landed at another airfield, or crash-landed in the sea, or . . ."

"I know," Mike said. "They might turn up. But I think if they'd landed somewhere else there'd have been a phone call by now. We'll go to the Operations Room in a minute to ask again."

But there had been no phone message, nothing reported at all.

"The best thing you can do," Mike said as they walked away, "is to get yourself a knockout pill from the MO and get in a few hours' sleep."

"But then I might miss something. Surely there must be some news, from somewhere."

Mike compressed his lips and shook his head slowly. "Well, there might be. But . . ."

"It's early yet," Kay insisted, "only a matter of hours . . ."

She would not let herself start to think that David might have been killed, even though she knew that the whole crew would be officially posted as missing. Like Stephen. Their families would be told. But there was still hope at this stage – there *must* be. They might be in the North Sea in a dinghy, to be picked up later by Air Sea Rescue. They might have bailed out over Germany and been taken prisoner. That might be just about bearable, unlike the alternatives.

Mike urged Kay again to go and get a sleeping pill. Kay knew that he was trying his best and that he was missing out on his own sleep, so she fell in with the idea as far as going with Helen to the MO's door. She had no intention of complying; to take a sleeping pill would be to admit that David was dead, anaesthetising herself against the shock. She did not want anaesthesia: she wanted to be conscious in case news came, any news at all. As soon as Helen had gone off to her own billet, Kay went back to the airfield. She stood by the perimeter watching the ground crews working on the planes to prepare them for ops that night. Someone was painting a new yellow bomb on the side of E-Easy's cockpit to show that she had completed another operation. It was a day like any other day. Twenty-one men and three planes were missing from last night's mission, but life went on as usual. The fact that one of the missing airmen was David did not make any difference to Bomber Command.

It was a gusty spring day. The wind had dropped from the night-time gales and the sky was fresh blue, with cumulus cloud piled high like whipped cream; a skylark was singing above the airfield. The beauty of the day stung Kay's feelings to rawness. She thought of the conversation with David in the field beyond, going over and over what she had said until it was like a needle stuck in the groove of a gramophone record. Nothing could change the fact that she had picked an argument with David, quite unnecessarily; she had hurt and upset him, and now he was gone.

When she could bear it no longer, she turned and walked quickly away, not knowing where she was going. She had the whole day off duty, but she could not contemplate going off camp, and she could not contemplate staying.

"I'm sorry, Kay, really sorry, but honestly I've no idea at all what happened to them."

"Thanks, anyway," Kay said flatly.

Alistair Tait gave her a sympathetic glance and went off to his night flying test. He had at least been approachable, willing to tell her what he could. Some of the others had avoided her as if she were unlucky. She had pestered everyone she could find who had been on the raid, getting them to tell her whatever they could about it. Most of them confirmed what the New Zealander had said, that it had been an "absolute bloody shambles", with planes blown off course so badly that some had flown over the heavily defended Ruhr Valley. It was hardly surprising that no one knew what had happened to the missing aircraft. She continued to cling to the possibility that David's crew had bailed out or survived a crash landing and were alive somewhere in Germany, but none of the other crews had seen anything to confirm this or even to suggest it. For most of them, last night was a closed chapter; they were more concerned with their own chances of surviving tonight. One of the pilots had said, almost casually, "I'm sorry Evans got the chop. He was a decent bloke."

His use of the past tense made Kay feel sick. Aircrew had to get used to losses; you couldn't expect them to spend time grieving each time another crew failed to return. They had to develop a certain callousness. And Kay knew that she was just as callous herself: she had been prepared to accept any number of lost crews as long as David kept coming back, almost as if the loss of someone else improved the odds for his survival. She had sometimes appalled herself by the coldness of it, how much she had come to regard it as normal. And she had hardly spared a thought for the others in David's crew.

She went round to the crew room and asked to see the effects officer, spurred by some ridiculous hope that David had left a last loving message for her in his locker, something of himself for her to keep. It was common enough for aircrew to leave letters for wives or girl-friends, to be posted on if they went missing in action. But the officer looked blank.

"Flight Sergeant Evans. No, I'm pretty sure there was no letter."

Kay remembered that he would have had twenty other men's lockers to sort through that day and that David was just a name on his list. David's personal belongings would be packed up and sent to his home later if there were no news; Kay was officially nothing to do with him, not his wife or his fiancée. She walked away, suddenly overcome with weariness. She felt this disappointment as the final blow. Of course there had been no letter; she had been foolish to think there might be. David had no need to write her letters, as he saw her nearly every day. And if he had written one, any sentiments in it would have been out of date – she had seen to that herself, by spoiling their last meetings.

She should not have gone to the effects officer. The image of his empty locker, cleared of his possessions ready for the next newcomer, stayed with her. It was another of the official ways of pronouncing him dead.

She was too tired to haul herself round any longer. She went back to her room, hoping that Felicity would not be back, and got into bed.

The next few days dragged past. Kay went about her duties in a trance, the surface part of her brain coping with the routines, so that she was sometimes surprised to look at a neatly filled page in her log book and realise that she had written it herself. The punishment she had been given for breaking out of camp was discreetly forgotten. Mike and Helen told her to take compassionate leave, but she would not. She felt as if her work was the only thing holding her together. People were sympathetic, but sympathy was the last thing she felt able to cope with. She wanted everyone to treat her as if nothing had happened, for fear that she would start weeping and not be able to stop. She felt as if she were standing on the edge of a black abyss; if she let herself think that David was dead, she would fall into it and never get out.

"Oh God, Kay, how awful for you," Felicity said when she came back. "It would almost be easier for you if someone had seen them shot down. At least then you'd know."

She was right, in a way. Kay knew by now that she was alone in refusing to believe that David was dead. She had seen the guarded expression cross people's faces when she mentioned the possibility that he might be alive somewhere. There was a chance, but a slim one. And because no one had witnessed any of the various disasters which could have befallen K-King and her crew, it seemed to Kay that they had all happened, simultaneously. When she slept, she dreamed about the plane exploding in mid-air in a ball of flame, or screaming into a dizzying spiral from which no one could escape, or crashing into the sea with everyone trapped inside. She saw David dying slowly of exposure in a dinghy in the North Sea, or parachuting down to a violent death at the hands of irate Germans, eager to wreak vengeance for their own dead. Her reeling mind supplied endless possibilities, all of them unbearable. Sometimes she woke herself up with the sick hollowness of shock, but the pictures would not fade.

Felicity tried to be kind, but between them was the unspoken knowledge that Sandy Beacham could have been with his crew that night, and that the outcome might have been different if he had flown the plane. Kay hated him for still being alive. Felicity did not refer to the leave she had spent with him, and Kay did not ask about it. But it was difficult to go on sharing the room with Felicity. They began to avoid each other, and Kay wondered whether to ask for a change. The rift made her feel more lonely than ever; they had their differences of opinion, but Felicity had always been a cheering influence.

Kay wrote to her mother and to David's parents. They were not easy letters to write. Kay could imagine only too clearly the effects of the official *Missing* letter on David's kindly parents, who must have been dreading this since he had been flying on operations. She told them about David's commission, knowing how proud they would have been; David had almost certainly not had time to write to them about it himself.

Alice wrote back by return of post, offering to come up to Lincoln and spend a day or two with Kay. Kay replied, thanking her for the offer, but putting it off. She knew that Alice would understand her feelings exactly, having had an identical experience herself, but this would only make a meeting harder, not easier.

A Midsummer Night's Dream was due to be performed on Saturday of the next week. Charlie said he would cancel it.

"No," Kay said. "I'm going to do it. You can't get anyone else to be Hermia at such short notice and you can't let the others down after they've put so much into it."

"They don't mind scrubbing round it."

"Of course they would. Anyway, I'm going to be in it."

She didn't quite understand why it was so important to go ahead with it; something to do with pretending there was a glassy surface to skate across, keeping her from the yawning black hole. But she did not think she could explain this adequately to Charlie.

"I must do it," was all she said.

He looked at her and nodded slowly. "All right, then. If you're really sure."

He didn't sound at all sure himself, and she knew he was afraid that she'd rush off the stage in floods of tears in the middle of the performance. She was rather afraid of it herself. But she went to rehearsals as usual and played Hermia reasonably competently, and helped Larry to be a nastier Lysander in the quarrel scene. It was a kind of anaesthetic, and soon she would have to come round. But not yet.

PERFORMANCE

"*N*ow, fair Hippolyta, our nuptial hour draws on apace . . ."

Mike's opening words, as Theseus, sounded thin and hollow as they floated out over the audience. Kay waited in the wings, in her draped Grecian-style dress, with Larry and the two others who were to make their first entrance with her. Normally she would have felt nervous; tonight she just wanted to get on to the stage and get on with it. Playing Hermia was a way of stepping out of the real world for two hours. She was glad the performance had gone ahead; so much hard work had gone into it, from Charlie's patience as director to the beautiful backdrops painted by one of the transport staff.

". . . with pomp, with triumph, and with revelling."

It was their cue. Kay walked on sulkily, led by Egeus, her father, who appealed to Duke Theseus to forbid her from marrying Lysander and to make her marry Demetrius instead.

"Demetrius is a worthy gentleman," Mike said.

"So is Lysander." She had got her first line out without stuttering or drying up.

Larry's voice wobbled on his opening lines, but the first scene went smoothly enough and now it was the turn of the comic characters, led by Wally as Peter Quince and Charlie as Bottom. Kay knew that the audience would relax and enjoy the play as soon as Charlie came on. Those who had considered Shakespeare rather highbrow for their tastes were soon laughing helplessly as Bottom postured and gesticulated, offering to play all the parts in the labourers' entertainment, including the lion, and demonstrating a roar of blood-curdling ferocity. This scene was followed Max as Puck, the mischievous imp; he minced on in green tights, fake pointed ears and a short belted tunic with petalled edges, getting whoops and catcalls from the audience. Helena and Demetrius entered next, and soon they were into the confusion of Puck's magic potion being administered to the wrong people and all the lovers getting mixed up.

Kay knew that she was not giving her best

performance, but neither was she letting herself down, or the others in the cast. It was the best she had hoped for. She and Joyce delivered their quarrel with customary venom, the lovers' tangle was sorted out, and her speaking part was over. All she had to do in the final act was to sit on stage as a member of the wedding party and to enjoy the ham acting of the comic characters. Charlie was in his element; he staggered about the stage in theatrical passion, stabbing himself melodramatically and then reviving in order to enjoy his death scene to the full.

Kay laughed and applauded with the others, but now that her speaking part was over she felt the tension draining out of her and the black emptiness returning. After the curtain calls there was a party for the cast, with beer and sandwiches, and Charlie and Mike taking it in turns to play the piano. Kay could not face it. She changed out of her costume and cleaned off her make-up without saying much to Joyce and the other girls, taking her time. When they had gone out to the party she turned the light off and sat by herself on the sofa where she and David had sat so recently. She smoothed a hand over the worn velvet pile where David had sat. If she closed her eyes she could see him. Someone was playing *Easy Come, Easy Go* on the piano, with the others singing along. It was too much. She could not hold back the choking sobs any more, or stop the hot tears from spilling. The play had been a barrier between her and despair, but now it was gone and there was nothing left. She was letting herself wallow, but could not help it: she *needed* to wallow, after so much restraint. She would get up in a moment and go out of the side door, not wanting to spoil the party for the others.

The door opened and someone turned the light on. "Kay? Aren't you coming to have a drink?" It was Charlie.

"In a minute." She turned her head away so that he wouldn't see her crying, but Charlie took one look at her and then closed the door and came to sit beside her. It was no use trying to hide it; she sobbed with great shuddering breaths in a way she hadn't cried since she was a little girl. It was a force caged up in her and finally released, a wild thing that wanted to claw at her and tear her to pieces. She could do nothing but give herself over to it. At last she began to cry more quietly, and to get her breathing under control. She had almost forgotten about Charlie, but he was still there, saying nothing, occasionally stroking her arm.

"Sorry, Charlie," she said eventually, all stuffed up.

"It's all right. Any time."

"I didn't mean to spoil the party."

"You're not. I just noticed you weren't there, that's all."

She fumbled with her soaked handkerchief and blew her nose. "You must have been pleased . . ." she began, but her voice was quavering too much to continue.

"You don't have to make polite conversation," Charlie said. "Carry on and let it all out. You obviously need to. That was like the breaching of the ruddy Ruhr dams. The Lord only knows how you got through tonight."

"Oh, Charlie, I don't know what to do. It's so awful . . ."

"I know. I know it is."

It was a relief to find herself talking to someone. "I can't stand not knowing . . . And the waste of it, the awful waste! David and twenty others . . . The raid was a failure anyway, and he hated the idea of bombing Berlin . . . And, Charlie . . ."

"Go on."

"Have you got a spare handkerchief?"

He found his in his pocket and gave it to her.

". . . And what makes it even worse is that . . . is that . . . I was horrible to him, that last afternoon, before . . . We had an argument, just because he wanted me to put in for a commission, and I wouldn't . . . and he was being recommended for one and I didn't even congratulate him . . ."

Charlie nodded slowly. "And that was the last time you saw him?"

"Nearly . . . I went out to the airfield, just before take-off, and . . . I saw him for about two seconds . . . to say I was sorry."

"And what did he say?"

"He said it was all right, and not to worry and he'd . . . he'd . . ." She could not get the words out. She blew her nose and tried again. "He'd see me tomorrow . . ."

"Then I don't suppose it would have mattered one bit. Listen, Kay. It must be bloody difficult to be involved with a bloke who could get the chop any night he's on ops. Any time you have a bit of a barney, you know it could turn out like it did for you, and you're bound to think it was all your fault. It'd be easy for a bloke to take advantage of that."

"But David didn't . . ."

"No, I wasn't saying he did. But from what you said, it was just a run-of-the-mill tiff, like any girl and her bloke are bound to have now and then. It wouldn't have mattered. If he'd come back you'd have kissed and made up in no time."

Kay sniffed and pondered this for a few moments.

"I don't suppose I'll ever find out what happened to him."

It was the first time she had acknowledged it.

"No," Charlie said. "You probably won't."

He made it sound like a pronouncement. Her eyes brimmed over again.

"It's what you warned me about," she said. "I mean, I knew what might happen, so did David . . . of course we did. How could we not think about it when it's going on all around us, people not coming back? . . . but it doesn't make it any easier, not at all. Worse, if anything, because you've been expecting it, waiting for it . . . But it's bad form to make a fuss, isn't it? You're expected to take it on the jaw, treat it as part of your war effort . . . When I was on watch once, an officer came in and said to Roberts, 'Did you know old So-and-So's bought it,' and Roberts said, 'How did his wife take it?' and the first chap said, 'Like a thoroughbred.' Like a thoroughbred! What does that mean? Aren't women supposed to care? Are we meant to keep a stiff upper lip and say 'He died serving his country, the way he'd have wanted'? Well, I can't. Not when it's such an awful waste. I'm not a thoroughbred. I'm a human being." Her voice had risen with indignation and she stopped in surprise at her outburst.

Charlie was looking at her with mild amazement. "That was quite a speech."

She mopped at her eyes with the damp handkerchief.

"You're not married, are you, Charlie?" She had never heard him speak of a wife or girl-friend at home.

"Not me, no. Footloose and fancy free."

"Did you ever love anyone?"

"Once. We were engaged, even had the date fixed for the wedding. Church booked and everything. Dorothy, her name was. And what did she do? Went off with a brown job, an army NCO. Married him instead. Two years ago, that was. They've got babies now. Twins."

"That must have been awful for you, being let down," Kay said.

Charlie shrugged stoically. "I got over it."

FELICITY

Kay and Felicity continued to see little of each other, apart from the rare occasions when their duties coincided. Both on and off duty, Kay became more friendly with Helen, whose undemanding presence suited her need for quiet companionship. Charlie arranged for two more performances of *A Midsummer Night's Dream* in the local village hall and on a nearby fighter station, and his cast began to feel like touring professionals. Before long Charlie began talking about a new project, a musical. Kay thought she would excuse herself from this one, but Charlie persuaded her that it was exactly what she needed to divert her from her misery: time-consuming rehearsals to fill her spare hours, and the company and banter of the cast.

Her relationship with Felicity had changed from friendship to awkward tolerance, at best, and Kay wondered again whether to ask for a change of room. But before she had got around to suggesting it, she became aware that Felicity was not her usual robust self. She looked pale and worried, and was not eating well; she gave curt replies to Kay's expressions of concern. One morning Felicity scrambled out of bed, left the room in a hurry and returned ten minutes later looking weak and shaken. She shot a reproachful glance at Kay, who was sitting up in bed, and got back under her blankets without saying anything.

"Felicity! Aren't you well?"

There was no answer. Kay got out of bed and shook her shoulder. "Please answer! You're ill, aren't you? It's no good going on duty like this. Why don't you go over to Sick Quarters and report ill?"

Felicity's answer was a mumble beneath the blankets. "I'm not ill. There's nothing the MO can do for me."

"But you are! You're pale, you're not eating properly, you look awful . . ."

Felicity rolled over and looked at Kay with angry blue eyes.

"Thanks a lot. That's just what I need."

"Why are you being so obstinate?" Kay retreated to sit on her own bed. "Why won't you admit that you're not well and you need a few days off?"

Felicity smiled wryly. "Kay, you're so naive. Anyone else would have guessed by now."

"Guessed what?" Kay said, thinking that perhaps Felicity was suffering from some malignant disease which could not be treated.

"I'm not ill," Felicity said. "I'm pregnant."

She said it so matter-of-factly that Kay was shocked into silence. She stared at Felicity, who continued to gaze at the ceiling as if finding something interesting written there.

"Go on," Felicity said. "Say something."

"I thought—"

"You thought I could take care of myself? Yes, so did I. It was a mistake, a silly mistake. Well, I've got what I deserve, I suppose. You can say it if you like."

"But what are you going to do? Have you told Sandy? It *is* his baby?"

"Yes, of course it's his," Felicity said huffily. "I may be flighty but I don't sleep with more than one man at a time. And no, I haven't told him."

"But you will?"

"I don't know. I haven't told anyone yet. Only you, now."

"What are you going to do?"

Felicity began to cry quietly. "I don't know. I really don't know."

Kay went to her and sat on the edge of the bed and tried to comfort her. Beneath her concern for Felicity was an acute sense of irony – that Felicity had conceived a baby, on the same night, perhaps, that David had gone missing; that Sandy Beacham had been creating a new life, instead of dying with his crew . . . It was more than she could cope with. She fought back her own tears, and found a handkerchief for Felicity.

"Are you sure you're pregnant? You couldn't be mistaken?"

Felicity sat up and blew her nose. "I've missed one period. But I'm sure. Feeling sick, and everything – What else could it be?"

"Shouldn't you see a doctor, to make sure?"

"Oh yes," Felicity said, reviving enough to be sarcastic, "go to the MO and say 'I think I'm pregnant, by a flight lieutenant.' That would go down a treat, wouldn't it?"

"But you need to look after yourself – eat properly, and get regular rest, all that sort of thing."

"Good grief, Kay, you'll be knitting baby socks next. You don't imagine I'm going to be walking around camp eight months pregnant, do you, with the Queen Bee encouraging me to take it easy and put my feet up?"

"No." Kay stared at her bare toes on the cold lino. "What will you do? Go home to your parents?"

Felicity started to cry again. "God, no. That's the last thing I'd think of doing. You don't know my parents. I couldn't tell them. They'd kill me, absolutely disown me . . . I've always been a disappointment to them. I couldn't bear for them to know, I'd be terrified to tell them. They'd see it as a disgrace for the whole family. They wouldn't have me in the house. Oh, Kay, I don't know what to do. It's such a mess . . ."

"I'll help you. I'll help you however I can," Kay said, feeling completely out of her depth. What *could* she do to help? Although she had known that Felicity did not get on well with her parents, she could not imagine what it would be like not to be able to go home with problems. She realised that she was infinitely luckier than Felicity. Her own mother would never turn her away, or disown her, whatever she had done. Even if she had returned home in Felicity's condition, Alice would have supported her; she might even be pleased. But Alice did not care much for convention, as Felicity's parents obviously did, and the idea of disgrace would not enter her head. Stop thinking about it, Kay told herself sharply. It was irrelevant. David was gone, and he had never had the chance to father a child. It was no good thinking of the what-ifs and the if-onlys, Kay thought, remembering Uncle Jack. The immediate problem was waiting to be solved. Felicity's pregnancy would soon become apparent and something would have to be done. Felicity would have to leave the WAAF, or be dismissed. In spite of their recent aloofness with each other, Kay did not want her to go.

"You must tell Sandy about it," Kay said. "And soon. It's only right that he should know."

"I suppose so." Felicity did not sound keen.

"He might be pleased. Perhaps you'll get married." She wondered why Felicity had not mentioned the possibility. It would be a solution to the problem with her parents, if she made a respectable marriage to an officer. She pictured the wedding: Felicity radiant, Sandy in uniform, smiling parents, a guard of honour. "Do tell him, Felicity. It's not right for you to worry about it on your own. It's his responsibility as well."

"All right. Thanks, Kay, for listening. Move over, I'm getting up. I'm on duty in half an hour." Felicity swung her legs out of bed and stood up. With a speed of recovery which astonished Kay, she looked at herself in the mirror and said briskly. "God, I look a fright, not fit to be seen. I must make myself presentable."

When Kay went on duty later, Mike told her that his posting had come through, and that he would be going out to the Middle East. She received the news gloomily, and wondered whether she should apply for a posting herself in a month or two. Felicity would have to leave, one way or another, and now Mike as well. Charlie would be disappointed, too, to lose a key member of his performing troupe. Kay felt as if her life had been turned upside down in the last few weeks. Perhaps I need a change too, she thought; I've been here long enough. But it would be a difficult decision to make. She felt oddly attached to the airfield and the ever-changing Lincolnshire sky; in spite of everything, she would be reluctant to leave. Soon, perhaps, she would ask to move on, but not yet. She could not face the idea of severing her link with David, or the effort of starting again with a group of strangers. And first there was Felicity's problem to be sorted out.

Felicity asked Kay to go out for a walk with her next time they both had an evening free. As soon as they had booked out at the main gate, Felicity filled her lungs with air and then let her breath out in a long gusty sigh. "I just had to get out for an hour or two. Where shall we go? You know where the walks are."

Kay led her down a dusty farm track between beet fields. It was a mild spring evening; the stream beside the track was fringed by grey-green willows, with celandines flowering in the hollows. A willow warbler poured out its silvery descending tune in the tree canopy. Kay paused to listen, but Felicity was not a nature lover and neither was she much of a walker. Kay knew that the walk was an excuse to talk about Felicity's dilemma, well away from camp.

"Something's really going to happen this time, isn't it?" Felicity said, avoiding the obvious topic. "The roads have been full of traffic going south."

"Yes. It's in the air, on the station and outside. It's the first time I can remember people being optimistic in this whole dreary war."

Everyone in Lincoln and the village seemed to be expecting the invasion of France, discussing it in hushed tones as if German spies might be lurking in the nearest shop doorway or between the potato plants. Bomber Command was gearing itself up for something special, too. Shiny new Lancasters were coming up from the factories with their paint barely dry, and the ground crews worked long hours to get all the older ones serviceable. New crews arrived, fit and keen; in the warm spring sunshine they played cricket or lay on the grass outside the flight offices, waiting for news of ops. Night-time operations were heading south to France to bomb railway lines and bridges in order to impede German troop movements. The invasion was definitely coming this time, after two years of rumours and false reports, but no one knew where or when.

Kay and Felicity walked for some distance across the fields before Felicity said, halfway across a rickety footbridge, "I told Sandy."

"Yes?" Kay stopped at the other end to look round at her, but Felicity carefully avoided meeting her eye.

"It's no good, Kay. I know you thought he'd do the decent thing and offer to marry me, and all my problems would be over. But it's not on. I've got to sort it out by myself."

"Why? What did he say?" Kay said indignantly. "Doesn't he think he's at all responsible?"

"Oh yes. But there's not much he can do, really."

"Why not?" Kay said, appalled. "What do you mean, there's not much—"

Felicity picked her way carefully across the bridge and walked slightly ahead. "He can't marry me, you see," she said, "because he's married already."

"Felicity—"

"I didn't know, honestly I didn't. He didn't tell me, not before." Felicity looked at Kay, her face flushed and defiant. "He said he would have married me if he could."

"Oh, very decent of him! I suppose that

helps? So what's he going to do – go back to his wife and leave you in the lurch?"

"He's not as bad as you think," Felicity protested.

"Isn't he?" Kay flared back.

They walked all the way across a pea field, their shoes brushing against the young plants, before either spoke again. Then Felicity said, "Look, it's over now between me and Sandy. Such as it ever was. I know you haven't actually said it serves me right, but I know you think it."

"That's not fair," Kay objected. "I haven't said anything of the sort."

"But you do think it. I know you do."

"All right then – I don't know how you could have been so casual about it, if you want to know. But it's too late to argue about that now. It isn't just you and Sandy any more, is it? There's a new life; a baby to be thought about and provided for. It's what happens next that we've got to decide. When you've stopped making excuses for Flight Lieutenant Beacham."

"I'm not making excuses," Felicity snapped. "I'm trying to be honest. Can't you see that? I'm not some wronged maiden from a folk ballad. It was my fault just as much as his. I met him halfway. More than halfway, perhaps."

Kay relented. "Oh, God, what a mess. Well, yes, you *are* being honest, but the fact remains that he didn't tell you he was married and now he's going to carry on just as he is. Men can. Women can't."

"I know." Felicity stared bleakly across the fields. "I'm going to have to leave the WAAF before anyone finds out. Can you imagine Bellyache's face if she gets the chance to parade me in front of the Queen Bee for the sack?"

"But where will you go? Are you still set against going home?"

"I told you, I wouldn't go home if it were the last place on earth, and I meant it. I'll go anywhere but there."

Kay climbed the stile slowly and sat down on the top rail, thinking hard. She did not know how Felicity could be so calm about it; the problems facing her seemed overwhelming. She had no idea what to suggest. What was the official WAAF policy on unmarried mothers? Surely Felicity wouldn't be thrown out to fend for herself?

She said, "Look, there's only one way I can think of to help, and that's to write to my mother. She helps run a shelter in the East End. I know she'd help you."

"I don't want charity, thanks," Felicity said. She gestured for Kay to get off the stile so that she could come over. "You make me sound like Fanny Robin crawling to the workhouse. I'll find somewhere for myself."

DOMESTIC NIGHT

Wednesday night was the hated Domestic Night, when every WAAF not on duty was expected to be in her quarters polishing her buttons and mending her uniform. The WAAFs resented this intrusion into their free time, as they had plenty of spare hours in which to do the necessary jobs. The airmen didn't have a Domestic Night; it was just for the women. Kay suspected that it was intended to prepare them for being good little wives after the war. She walked back from the mess thinking about the letter she was going to write to her mother. One advantage of sharing the room with Felicity instead of being quartered in the more public Nissen hut was that she could carry on with writing or reading, leaving her sewing kit and a pair of holey stockings ready on the bed to be snatched up when she heard the tread of the admin officer outside.

As soon as she entered the room she guessed what had happened. Felicity's bed was unusually tidy, biscuits and blankets stacked in orthodox fashion, no clutter of hairpins and make-up on the locker. Her greatcoat was still hanging on the door peg with Kay's, but that was all. Kay went to the locker and found it unfastened and empty. There were no personal belongings left at all. Felicity had gone without even leaving a note.

Kay heard the main door opening and closing and Bellingham's voice outside, talking loudly to the WAAF corporal. Their footsteps went down the corridor: they were starting at the other end, fortunately. Kay quickly got out her sewing kit and put it on Felicity's bed, to look as if Felicity were about to come back. She threw her own pair of stockings down beside it, got out her button stick and polish and sat down demurely on the upright chair to clean her buttons and badges. Her thoughts raced: she did not know what to do.

Bellyache marched in without knocking. "Evening, Leary." Her glance flicked over to Felicity's vacant place. "Where's Whiting? She's not on duty tonight, is she?"

"I don't think so," Kay said, knowing that

Bellingham could easily check the rota.

"Well, where is she, then?"

"I don't know. Perhaps she's on her way over from the cookhouse," Kay hedged.

"Did you see her there?"

"No, but it was very crowded."

Bellingham's eyes gleamed in anticipation. Kay knew that she did not like Felicity, regarding her as potential trouble. Well, Felicity was in trouble all right, but Kay was not going to let Bellingham know if she could help it.

"I shall have to put her on a charge if she's absent for Domestic Night without a good reason," Bellingham said with relish. She turned to the pudding-faced corporal who stood in the doorway behind her. "I'll look back in when I've finished the rounds."

She closed the door firmly, and Kay continued polishing, wondering what to do now. Felicity's absence could not be concealed for long. It occurred to her that perhaps Felicity had been to see Section Officer Cummings and had asked for a discharge, but she rejected this idea as soon as she had thought of it. Felicity was under twenty-one, still her parents' responsibility according to WAAF regulations; if she had told Mrs Cummings she was pregnant, her parents would have been informed automatically. That wasn't Felicity's way. She was stubbornly independent, determined to sort things out by herself. But what could she do? She had no ration book, and her money would soon run out. Kay supposed she might find a civilian job in munitions or aircraft production and carry on working for a few more months, but then how would she cope as an unmarried mother with a new baby?

Before the evening was out Kay found herself summoned to Section Officer Cummings' office. Waiting in the corridor outside and inhaling the strong smell of floor polish, she remembered last time she had spoken to Mrs Cummings, facing her charge of breaking out of camp. David had never had to answer his charge . . . It was only a matter of weeks ago. It seemed like years, and like yesterday.

Section Officer Cummings called her in. Kay was relieved to find that there was no one else present, no Bellingham to gloat. But she had no idea what she was going to say. If only it were as easy as facing a charge and being given a simple punishment . . .

She saluted, and Mrs Cummings said, "At ease, Leary. Do sit down."

"Thank you, ma'am."

"I'm sure you know why I asked to see you. Flight Sergeant Bellingham reported that Air-craftwoman Whiting was absent at Domestic

Evening without reason, and that all her belongings seem to have been taken away."

"Yes, ma'am."

"Do you know where she is?"

"No, ma'am."

"Do you think she may have gone on leave without a pass? Or does she not intend to return?"

"I don't know. I haven't seen her since this morning and she said nothing about going. She didn't leave a message for me. I don't know where she is."

"Do you think she'll have gone home to her parents?"

Kay hesitated. "I don't think so. She doesn't get on well with them."

Mrs Cummings was silent for a few moments, tapping her pen on the desk. Then she said, "I shall have to notify them, of course, if she doesn't return. Has she got a particular boyfriend? Someone on the station?"

"No, ma'am,' Kay lied. "She goes out with lots of different people. No one special."

She was not sure why she did not tell Mrs Cummings about Sandy Beacham: she saw no reason why he should be protected. Her instinct was to avoid making things worse for Felicity, but how could they be worse than they already were?

"So you've really no idea at all where she may

231

be." Mrs Cummings looked penetratingly at Kay, as if suspecting that she knew more than she chose to reveal.

"No, ma'am, I haven't," Kay said, truthfully enough.

"I shall expect you to let me know, or Flight Sergeant Bellingham, if you hear anything, or if she contacts you," Mrs Cummings said.

"Yes, ma'am." The discussion seemed to be over. Kay stood up and saluted and was about to leave, when Mrs Cummings called her back.

"I was sorry to hear about Flight Sergeant Evans, Leary," she said quietly. "Very sorry indeed. I know you must be having an extremely difficult time."

Kay thanked her and escaped, relieved to get out of the office without bursting into tears. She found sympathy difficult to cope with. At least Felicity's predicament had made her think about someone else's problems rather than her own. Wearily, she leaned on the brick wall outside the building and collected her thoughts. She was not at all sure that she had done the right thing. If only Felicity had left a note saying where she had gone, and whether she planned to come back! It would have made deception so much easier.

"Smarten up, Leary," Flight Sergeant Bellingham said sharply, coming out of the door behind her.

*   *   *

When Kay saw Sandy Beacham walking towards the Officers' Mess with another flight lieutenant, she went straight up to him and saluted.

"Could I have a word with you, sir?"

Sandy Beacham, in mid-conversation, broke off and looked at her in some surprise. "Yes, what is it?"

"I need to talk in private," Kay said.

The other officer's face expressed mild amusement, as if he had stumbled upon a romantic attachment. He raised one eyebrow and said, "See you in the bar then, Sandy."

Kay waited until he was out of earshot and then said bluntly, "It's about Felicity. Do you know where she is?" She wished she didn't find him quite so intimidating, with his formidable self-assurance and his DFC, but she couldn't keep calling him "sir", under the circumstances.

Sandy Beacham looked down at her haughtily. "I'm afraid I've no idea," he said. "Where would she usually be at this time of day?" He might have been speaking of some distant acquaintance.

"She's disappeared," Kay said. "No one knows where she is, and I've just had to lie to the WAAF CO about it."

His light blue eyes regarded her warily. She realised that he was wondering how much she knew. To speed things up, she said, "Felicity's told me about being pregnant. Now she's gone off somewhere and I've no idea where. She must be desperate. You've got to help."

"I don't see how I can." Sandy's gaze slithered past her face. She saw his embarrassment at being accosted like this by a mere ACW. "I've told you that I don't know where she is. I gave her some money. There's not much else I can do."

"Is that all?" Kay said. "She's carrying your child, and you're going to give her money, and that's all you can do? I suppose now you can forget all about her—"

She was amazed to find herself talking so boldly to an officer on such a delicate matter. If she had planned it first, she wouldn't have had the nerve to confront him.

Sandy looked at her coldly. "It's none of your business, Kay. I suggest that you go away and stop flinging accusations about. It's between me and Felicity. She's a consenting adult—"

"But you weren't fair to her – she didn't know you were married!"

He took hold of her arm in a strong grip. She resisted, but he led her away from the path which led to the Officers' Mess. He had recovered from his surprise at being wrong-footed and he spoke to her in the manner of an officer used to giving orders and having them obeyed.

234

"I really can't have you following me about and speaking to me like this in front of anyone who happens to come along. Use your common sense, for goodness' sake. Do you want to make things worse for all of us? I know you're concerned for Felicity, and of course so am I, but since she's run off there doesn't seem to be much for either of us to do at present. If she comes back, or contacts me again, then I'll certainly give her whatever money she needs."

"Money!" Kay could not conceal her disgust. "That isn't going to solve anything! How can Felicity buy her way out of trouble? Perhaps you can, but she can't!"

"Don't be such a child," Sandy said scornfully. "Do you think Felicity doesn't need money? She needs to stay somewhere, and eat, doesn't she? I don't know what else you expect me to do. Resign my commission? Go and tell the station commander all about it? I really don't see how that would help Felicity, do you?"

"If you're so anxious to provide for her," Kay retorted, "then you'd better start thinking about the child she's carrying, as well. She's going to need money for a long time, to bring up a child on her own."

Sandy stared at her, tight-lipped, as if she were an impudent schoolgirl who had gone too far. "I don't need your advice. I've already told you, it's none of your business. Now go away. I know you've lost your boyfriend and I'm sorry about it – David was a good lad – but don't use it as an excuse to behave in this hysterical manner. I shall tell you if I hear from Felicity, but apart from that I don't intend to discuss it again. You'll attract attention."

"That would be inconvenient, wouldn't it?" Kay said. It was a limp answer, but she had no chance to say any more. Sandy walked away abruptly and turned the corner to the front door of the Officers' Mess, where he would probably dismiss her from his thoughts over a whisky at the bar. She was trembling with anger and frustration; all the things she should have said crowded into her head, as they always did after an argument. Apart from everything else, she was enraged by his patronising reference to David as *a good lad*. David may have been less experienced in all sorts of ways, but he was worth a hundred of Beacham, a thousand, she thought fiercely: whatever had Felicity seen in him?

As soon as she had time to go into Lincoln on the bus, Kay went to the post office and asked for the Leicester telephone directory. There were four Whitings listed, among them Col. R. Whiting, The Old Manse. This seemed the most likely of the four addresses shown to match Felicity's description of a large house.

Kay counted out her pennies, went into the telephone kiosk and asked the operator to connect her.

"You're through, caller. Put your money in now."

Kay pressed button A, and heard a female voice saying, "The Old Manse."

"Could I speak to Mrs Whiting, please?"

"Who shall I say is calling?" said the voice.

Kay gave her name. After such an age that she thought her time would run out she heard another, older voice saying, "Mrs Whiting speaking. Who is this?"

It was what Kay thought of as a tweed-suited voice, a country land owner's voice, someone not used to being bothered by casual callers.

"My name is Kay Leary," Kay said. "I'm in the WAAF at Windersby, with Felicity."

"I see," the voice said, managing to convey disapproval in the two words. "Is this a social call, or do you have some administrative role in the WAAF?"

"A social call. I'm a friend of Felicity's. I wondered whether she was at home."

"My daughter is not at home, and is not expected to be." There was a rising note at the end of the phrase, which Kay interpreted as "What business is it of yours?"

"Have you heard from her in the last few days?" she persevered.

There was an affronted pause, then Mrs Whiting said curtly, "I have not been in contact with my daughter, nor she with me, since she joined the WAAF. Nor do I expect to be contacted by other aircraftwomen –" she made it sound like an insult – "which I assume you must be. Goodbye, Miss . . . Leary."

Kay heard the receiver being replaced. She left the post office feeling as if she had been up before the WAAF CO on another charge. Except that Felicity's mother sounded far more formidable than Section Officer Cummings. What an awful woman, she thought – not even asking how Felicity was, or why I wanted to know! Felicity wasn't exaggerating after all when she said she wouldn't even think of going home. Imagine telling such an unmotherly mother that you were pregnant! The WAAF was only suitable for a certain type of girl, she remembered Felicity saying – to go home in her condition would be to give her parents the satisfaction of being proved right.

Kay had one or two small purchases to make in Lincoln. She wandered down the main shopping street deep in thought, feeling that the phone conversation had explained something about Felicity. Perhaps Felicity's need for attention and admiration from various men was her way of making up for the lack of love from her parents. But Kay was no nearer to knowing where Felicity had gone, and could not think how to find out. After a few days she guessed that Section Officer Cummings must have contacted Felicity's parents about her disappearance. Kay wondered whether Mrs Whiting would be concerned, even then.

Kay had written to the International Red Cross and to the Air Ministry for news of David, and she knew that if he had been taken prisoner she would be unlikely to hear for at least a month to six weeks afterwards. So far, all she had received was a letter from the Red Cross saying that there was no information, and one from the Air Ministry: . . . *as soon as any definite news is received you will be informed. The Air Council desire me to convey to you their sympathy in your present anxiety*. But nothing more. Every day was a fresh disappointment. David's possessions had been returned to his parents, who had written to Kay sending her two photographs: one of herself which David had taken at New Year, and one of him in uniform. He was laughing, looking straight at the camera. It filled her with such an ache of longing for him that she could hardly bear to look at it, but she kept it by her bedside all the same.

There was no doubt at all now that the invasion of France was going to take place. Each day, the sky was loud with aircraft flying south;

planes of all types, American Flying Fortresses as well as RAF fighters and bombers, many towing gliders. Crews who returned from ops in France reported seeing an armada of ships crossing the Channel, and radios all over camp were permanently switched on for the latest news. On the evening of June 6th there was complete silence in the mess as everyone's ears were tuned to the six o'clock news, with eye witness accounts from the French beaches. Kay had heard rumours that the invasion would take place in the Calais area, but more than a hundred thousand troops had landed in Normandy, with an umbrella of aircraft providing almost complete immunity from the Luftwaffe. Over the next few days, every newspaper in the village was bought up by early morning, and Kay and Helen went into Lincoln on their afternoon off to see the cinema newsreels. For the first time Kay felt that the end of the war was a real possibility; the Germans were being pushed back daily as more and more French towns and villages were liberated.

Alistair Tait had got into the habit of dropping into the Flying Control Office at odd times, as several of the aircrew did, and shortly after the D-Day landings he asked Kay to go out to dinner with him as a celebration. She refused, surprised that he had asked: he knew of her involvement with David. But next day he tried again.

"No messing about, I promise. Just a friendly evening out. I thought you could do with cheering up. You've looked so low lately."

He was so nice about it that she thought there was no harm in accepting.

"But he's an officer," Helen said, impressed, when Alistair had left. "Aren't you afraid you'll get caught?"

"Not really," Kay said, remembering that her reaction had been just like Helen's when Felicity had started going out with an officer, not so long ago. Then, she had thought it an act of extreme daring and defiance to break the rules. Now she didn't really care. If she were caught she'd be put on a charge, that was all. Nothing to be bothered about.

Alistair took her to the White Hart, next to the Cathedral Close. It was smarter and more expensive than the places she had been to with David, and seemed unlikely to be invaded by hordes of noisy aircrew. She was glad it wasn't one of their old haunts; it would be too poignant to return with someone else. Alistair seemed quite at ease in these surroundings, used to the attentions of receptionists and waitresses. It was part of being an officer, Kay supposed. She guessed that he had been out with lots of girls. She knew that several of the WAAFs would have envied her at this moment: Alistair was a conspicuous figure around the airfield, with his lanky height and his successful flying record and his attractive lopsided grin. During the meal he told her about his home near Edinburgh on his parents' farm, and his sister: "One of the first girls to get pilot's wings."

Kay was impressed. "Is she one of those women who flies the new planes up from the factories?"

"That's right. A damned good flier, too. You should see her bring a Lanc in to land. She knocks spots off some of the chaps."

He told Kay a little more about the raid on which David had gone missing. "It's gone down in aircrew history as the night of the big winds. I almost had a row with my navigator about it. He told me he was getting a wind speed of a hundred and thirty miles an hour, and I told him not to be such a fool. But he was right."

Kay was silent. She pictured David wrestling with his bearings and computations in the loneliness of his blacked-out position, the only member of the crew who could guide the plane safely to the target and back . . . She deliberately stopped herself from thinking of what disaster might have struck; she had imagined it all so many times, with infinite variations. She could not allow herself to think of it now. There had been no more raids to Berlin since, which struck her as bitterly ironic. And six nights later there had been a disastrous raid to Nuremberg, with even heavier losses.

She was disconcerted when Alistair started talking about Sandy Beacham, telling her how he had got his DFC last summer. "He brought back his Lanc absolutely crippled. One wing was half shot away and the tail was hanging off and one of the remaining engines pouring fuel. No one thought he could land it. The rest of the crew bailed out over the airfield except the wireless op who was too badly wounded. Otherwise, Sandy could have bailed out himself – the kite was obviously going to be a write-off. But he insisted on landing it to save the wireless op, even though everyone watching thought it'd go up in flames. He managed it somehow and got out with just a few scratches. And the poor old W/Op died anyway."

Kay could not join in Alistair's admiration of Sandy Beacham, in spite of his undoubted bravery. Instead, she told him of her hope that David may be alive somewhere in a prisoner-of-war camp. He listened sympathetically, and did not tell her that she was being silly and that she ought to face up to the fact that David was probably dead, as others had done. She almost wished she could have told him about her concern for Felicity as well.

They caught the late bus back to camp, taking care to report to the Guard Room several minutes apart, and Kay went back to her room reflecting that she had had a pleasant evening, with no need at all to feel disloyal to David.

That night Sandy Beacham flew on the final operation of his second tour, and went on leave. Within a few days Kay heard that he had volunteered to join the Pathfinder Force and had been promoted to Squadron Leader.

Wonderful news! Alice wrote, a few days later. *Stephen has come back! Apparently his plane was shot down by a fighter near the German border but he managed to land it with himself and one other on board – the others bailed out and he doesn't know what happened to them. They managed to get over the border into France and made contact with Resistance workers who helped them to get down to the south and across into Portugal. From there, they got a ship back to England. Stephen had a broken arm which set badly through lack of attention, so he won't be able to fly again. But at least he's safe! He's in Ireland now with Jack and Sarah and Mary, and when he goes back he'll have some sort of ground job, in Intelligence, he thinks. I know you have been hoping to hear the same sort of news about David; if only you could . . .*

Kay read the letter again, doubly cheered. For Stephen, and because it was possible; she wasn't foolish to keep hoping . . . David could be somewhere in France at this very moment, helped by the Resistance workers he had wanted to support . . . and with Allied troops now in France, escape would become easier. She wrote to Stephen to congratulate him, hoping that she could meet him when he returned to England, to hear more about his enterprise. How wonderful for Uncle Jack and Aunt Sarah, and Stephen's wife . . . Miracles could happen, after all . . .

For some reason she found herself remembering a conversation she had had with David on one of their visits to Lincoln Cathedral. She had asked him whether he believed in God, and David had said that he ought to, coming from a Methodist family. "But no, I don't," he had said. "Only in the way that a lot of aircrew probably find that they do, over the Ruhr. I'll be a good boy if you'll just let me get my feet back on the ground . . . that sort of thing. Instant, temporary conversion."

Kay didn't believe in God either, any more than her mother had been able to believe in a God who had let thousands be slaughtered in the Great War. But it was easy to be superstitious, to try to make bargains. *I'll believe in you for ever and ever, if you'll just let me have David back.*

LEAVE

Kay was letting herself in at the front door of the accommodation block when she heard a rush of footsteps and someone scuttled in behind her.

"Felicity!" Kay exclaimed.

"Don't look so shocked. I'm not a ghost," Felicity said calmly.

"You gave me a fright – What are you doing? Where have you come from? Why didn't you tell me where you were?"

"Let's go in, and I'll tell you all about it."

Kay was surprised to see that Felicity was correctly turned out in her best blue, as if nothing had happened.

"Er . . ." Kay halted at their own door. "I had to take what was left of your kit back to the store. Everyone thought you'd gone for good –

so did I! Someone else lives here now. Helen, you know, from the Watch Office."

"Oh, it's all right," Felicity said off-handedly. "I'm only here for one night."

"Felicity, what's happened?"

They went in and Felicity sat down on the hard chair and looked at the photograph on the locker of Helen and her young brothers. Kay saw that she looked tired and pale, in spite of her carefully applied make-up.

"When I reported to the Guard Room, the admin officer there said she was putting me on a charge for not having a leave pass. I said not to worry, I was putting myself on a charge, and asked to see the WAAF CO."

"And did you see her? What did you say?"

"I just said that I'd had to go on leave to sort out a personal problem. I didn't say what it was. You know what Mrs Cummings is like, Kay, she's so reasonable that she makes you feel far worse than someone who hits you with the rule book."

"But . . . how much longer can you stay on? Shouldn't you have taken the chance to tell her about . . ."

"Oh, I'm staying on in the WAAF." Felicity examined a fingernail. "I've been demoted to General Duties. Spud bashing, I suppose that'll mean. What I expected to be doing in the first place." She gave Kay an unconvincing grin.

"I'm being posted to a WAAF training centre in Blackpool. I'm to go on the first transport bus in the morning, to catch the train. I've proved myself unreliable, haven't I? If I'm a very, very good girl and stay out of trouble, I might get back to flying control duties again."

"But—" Kay did not understand. She wondered for a moment whether Felicity had lost her grip on reality. "You can't pretend for much longer! Wouldn't it have been better to tell her you're going to have to leave anyway in another couple of months? And where have you been, all these days?"

Felicity did not answer for a moment. She picked up a book from Helen's locker and examined its cover. Then she looked at Kay and said matter-of-factly, "I'm not pregnant any more. I got rid of it. I had an abortion. I've been staying in London with friends while I – while I got over it."

Kay sat down on her bed, too shocked to say anything at all. Of all the surprises Felicity had given her recently, this was the most devastating.

Felicity gave her a sidelong glance. "I suppose you think I shouldn't have done it?"

A variety of responses chased themselves around Kay's head. "I don't know. I don't know. Where did you go to have it done?" she hedged. "Was it awful?"

Felicity pulled a face. "Well, it wasn't very pleasant. I went to a back-street clinic. Sandy gave me the money."

"He *knew* you were going to do it? He *knew* where you were, all the time?" Kay quickly reviewed her conversation with Sandy. Of course he had known. That was why he had treated her as a naive child, interfering.

"There wasn't much choice, really, was there?" Felicity said defensively. "Neither of us wanted it. It would have been impossible. Don't you think it was better this way?"

"But to give you the money, and send you off to go through that on your own . . ."

"All right, you don't have to rub it in," Felicity said. "It was a mess, and this was the easiest way out. It's over now. I've got a chance to start again. A baby – it would have been ghastly. I'd have been a hopeless mother."

Kay could see that it had been traumatic for her. Her blue eyes were edgy and strained; she had lost the healthy, self-aware sleekness which had been part of her attractiveness. Kay had little idea how an abortion was carried out, but she was sure it must be both distressing and painful. She felt a renewed surge of anger against Sandy Beacham for his casual handling of the matter.

"Sandy's not here any more," she said. "He finished his tour."

"Yes," Felicity said. "Well. I wasn't planning to see him again, I told you that." She glanced up at Kay. "What would you have done, if it had been you?"

"Good grief, I don't know," Kay said miserably. But she did. She reacted instinctively against abortion. If she had somehow found herself pregnant by David, she could no more have killed their child than she could have killed David; whatever the problems, she would have faced them. But she knew that her circumstances were very different from Felicity's. She and David loved each other; Felicity's relationship with Sandy had been no more than a casual affair, finished now. Her own mother would have given her every help; Felicity's parents would have disowned her. And how wise would it have been for Felicity to give birth to an unwanted child which she could not support? It was a tangled mess, from which Felicity had emerged in the most practical way available. It had clearly been an ordeal, and Kay felt sorry for her. But all the same she felt almost as angry with Felicity as she did with Sandy Beacham, for carelessly creating a baby and then ridding herself of it. It wasn't *right*, Kay felt strongly, to treat life and love so nonchalantly . . . She remembered saying, one night before Felicity had gone away, "Isn't it odd to think there are three of us in this room?"

and Felicity had said, "God, don't *say* that, Kay," as if she hated to think of the baby she was carrying as a living thing. Had she known then what she was going to do? She had not given the slightest hint, and it had never crossed Kay's mind.

Felicity stood up and stretched. "I'd better go back to the hut where they've parked me for the night. I'm supposed to have gone straight there."

Kay said, "I hope—" and then paused, not sure what she did hope. "Look after yourself," she said lamely, "and I hope you have better luck."

"And you, Kay. You're the one who needs better luck. Mine was just stupidity."

"Write to me when you get there."

"I will."

They hugged each other awkwardly. In spite of her mixed feelings, Kay wished that it didn't feel like a final parting.

Kay was due for a few days' leave before returning to take her ACW2 exam. She had been worried about her mother throughout the "Little Blitz" of renewed German bombing in the spring, and now London was facing a new threat – the pilotless flying-bombs, or "doodle-bugs" as some of the newspapers called them, fired from launching sites in the French coastal areas still occupied by German troops.

I think perhaps it would be best if you didn't come home next week after all, Alice wrote, just before Kay's leave, *with these renewed air raids. Could you put it off for a week or two, and see if the raids die down?*

Kay decided that she could be just as obstinate as her mother. *No, I'm coming!* she wrote back. *A few doodlebugs aren't enough to drive you away to Ireland, although goodness knows Uncle Jack's asked you there enough times, so they won't put me off either. Expect me and my gen-book – I've got another exam to revise for.*

Arriving at the flat, she found that Alice had someone staying with her: a young woman of perhaps nineteen or twenty, with a year-old baby boy. The mother, Mavis, had recently been made homeless when the block of flats she lived in had been devastated by a flying-bomb. She had already had to cope with the loss of her young husband, a naval rating, in the bombing of the troop ship *Rohna* off Algeria, the previous November. Alice had offered her a temporary home, although she told Kay that she was worried about keeping her there, in view of the continuing risk of raids.

"I wish I could get her out to the country somewhere," Alice said as they made up the camp bed for Kay, "but she doesn't want to go. All her friends are here."

Kay was a little disappointed not to have her

252

mother to herself, but meanwhile she had Mavis' company while Alice was at the children's clinic; sometimes they went shopping together or took the little boy to the park. He was a robust, lively child, apparently unmarked by trauma. Kay watched Mavis's patience with him, and could not imagine Felicity in such a role for a moment.

At the weekend, when Alice was off work, she and Kay went to a concert together and shopped, and went round to the rest centre, which was in fact in the school Kay had attended as a child, to help with meals. One evening they went down to the tube station to help with the WVS canteen there, serving soup and hot drinks to the people who had resumed the practice of sleeping underground to avoid the doodlebugs.

Mavis sometimes spent the night in the nearby public air raid shelter with her friends, but Alice stayed in the flat. Her only concession was to keep a torch and a whistle under her bed in case she was trapped in rubble. Nights spent lying awake after an air raid siren, listening for the angry buzz of flying bombs, made Kay realise how much the people of London had endured. She had escaped most of this, first during the Blitz and again now. She could never decide whether Alice's stoicism was amazingly brave or amazingly foolhardy; all she knew was that she felt compelled to match it. Alice would continue a conversation with barely a pause while a missile passed over and crashed further north-west, only breaking off if the explosion sounded close at hand.

"I'm sure these flying bombs tax everyone even more than the Blitz," she told Kay. "Coming as they do in the day time as well as at night. They make people feel helpless."

Kay was glad that the air raids on German cities had stopped, and she was able to tell Alice a little about the recent sorties to the flying-bomb sites in France – raids of a kind which even Alice could not object to, and which directly contributed to saving lives in England.

Broken nights, and the necessity of sharing a room since all Mavis's things were in Kay's bedroom, gave plenty of opportunity for talking. Kay read the letters Uncle Jack had sent about Stephen's escape and return home, and a letter from Stephen himself, and she showed Alice the correspondence about David from the Red Cross and the Air Ministry. Alice knew what it was like to be left in ignorance; she told Kay about the early days of the attack on Vimy Ridge, before she had heard about Edward, when she had known quite definitely that something had happened because there had been no word from him.

"And even after that," she said, "I heard two quite different reports about when he died, and how. I never really knew."

"It must have been odd," Kay said, staring into the darkness, "being married to my father, when you both knew that you'd have married Edward first if you'd had the chance."

"It was, in a way," Alice said, "but then Patrick and Edward had been close friends, too. We'd both lost him. Sometimes it was as if he was there, a third person in the marriage. But it was never a question of choosing between them, of loving one more than the other."

Kay listened to the black cat purring in the darkness on Alice's bed. Thinking of the china cat she had given David for luck, she reached up for her own good luck charm, the gold locket round her neck, which she always wore as she had promised him.

"I shan't ever get married," she said, "unless David does come back."

"I know you think that now," Alice said, "and whatever I say will sound middle-aged and cynical, but you're only eighteen . . . If David has gone, do you think he would have wanted you to spend the rest of your life in mourning? . . . Goodness!" She stopped in surprise.

"What?"

"Hearing myself . . . I sound just like Lorna did, telling me the same thing. And I can remember something else she said: 'You can't spend the rest of your life in love with a ghost.'"

"And did you believe her?"

"No," Alice said.

On the last afternoon of her leave, Kay went to buy food for the evening meal and then decided to walk round to the rest centre, where her mother usually called in on her way home from the clinic. The sun was warm on her back as she walked past the terraced houses with her shopping bag, thinking of what she would cook. When the air raid siren sounded, most people in the street reacted warily, rather than with any sign of panic; it was a tiresome interruption to everyday life, no cause for excitement unless something happened in the immediate vicinity. A loud buzzing like a vicious insect heralded the flight of a flying bomb overhead. People stopped and looked up at the sun, hands shielding their eyes from the glare, waiting for the intruder to go over harmlessly to land somewhere else. Then the buzzing stopped, and the plane-shaped bomb tipped nose-down and fell out of the sky, almost immediately overhead. Some people around Kay flung themselves down to the pavement but she stood paralysed as she watched it plummet and strike, two or three streets ahead of her, in the direction of the rest centre. The blast rocked her as it struck, and she saw pieces of debris flying into the air above the nearer rooftops, followed by a plume of dark smoke. People ahead of Kay ran to the scene, or picked themselves up and carried on with what they had been doing.

Kay ran too, on shaking legs, still clutching her shopping bag. *No, not Mum, not Mum*, pounded through her brain in rhythm with her feet. She rounded the corner of terraced houses and registered the devastation in the small square ahead. A large Victorian house had taken the impact; only a few fragments of wall stood upright, with floors and ceilings tipped at drunken angles and smashed remnants of furniture strewn about at random. The road in front was littered with broken glass and fragments of masonry, chimney stacks and roof tiles. There was no fire, but every window in the street seemed to have been blown out; shards of glass crunched under Kay's feet as she slowed her pace to take in the details. There were numerous casualties – bodies lay in the middle of the road, whether unconscious, or killed by the blast, she could not tell. *Not Mum, please not Mum . . .* it was a refrain in her head, a desperate plea; *not that, I couldn't bear it . . .*

She must keep calm. People in the street had

been hit by flying glass, and some of the less seriously hurt were being helped into houses by residents who had come out to help. The school building three doors along was intact, Kay saw with a gush of relief, although all its windows were broken. A wall on one side of the fruit and vegetable shop next to the Victorian house was partly caved in, and people were spilling out on to the street, clutching their heads or ears. The air was thick with explosive and brick-dust. Air raid wardens were trying to keep people out of the dangerously damaged building, and at the same time trying to find out from bystanders whether anyone was inside.

Kay knew that she must help the casualties. She was sagging with breathlessness, shock and relief, because the rest centre hadn't taken a direct hit as she had feared. She realised that she was still clutching the bag of groceries, and put it down on the glass-strewn pavement. Someone was clutching at her hand. She looked down to see a small girl of about eight gazing up at her, a frightened tear-stained face. Blood was flowing profusely from a long cut to the girl's free arm, the sleeve of her flowered dress ripped and soaking.

Kay crouched beside her. "I'll look after you. You'll be all right now."

From her basic training in first aid she knew that bleeding limbs should be raised above the level of the heart. She sat the little girl carefully on the pavement and held her arm up and pressed her fingers over the edges of the cut, looking around desperately for skilled help.

"Were you on your own? Or with your mummy?"

The child, sobbing, pointed towards the greengrocer's shop.

Kay looked in that direction. Customers who had been in the shop stood in huddles outside, amidst scattered bricks and glass and over-turned baskets of cabbages and plums. Rescue services were arriving: a heavy rescue team in a lorry loaded with wooden props and tunnelling equipment, getting as near as it could to the damaged house; a stretcher party, a grey auxiliary ambulance and a mobile first aid post. Their staffs immediately took over, swinging into a practised routine.

"Come on, let's find your mummy and get you bandaged up," Kay said to her charge. "What's your name?"

"Rosie Cooper, Flat 16, Drayman's Road," the child recited through her tears, well-trained. Kay picked her up and carried her frail weight to the aid post. She waited with the child and tried to stop the bleeding until a nurse could take over, and then explained that she was going to find the child's mother. She picked her way across to the greengrocer's, where the casualties were being briskly sorted from the merely frightened by a Red Cross nurse. Kay asked for Mrs Cooper. A frantic young woman with a badly cut face said, "Yes, that's me," and Kay pointed out where her daughter was.

Now she had to find her own mother. She saw that there had been fatalities in the Victorian house, as was almost inevitable; the stretcher party was carrying out the body of an elderly man, so coated in white dust that he looked like a stone figure in a cathedral crypt. Killed by blast, Kay thought; his face was so peaceful that she hoped he had known nothing about it. There would probably be others trapped or dead inside . . . Alice could have been walking along the street, instead of safely inside the school building . . . She could be one of the bodies shrouded in tarpaulin . . .

The walking wounded were being escorted into the school. Following, she saw that the rest centre was being used as a casualty post, leaving the ambulance to deal with the most serious injuries and get the victims off to hospital. Inside the school hall, Red Cross nurses were dealing with wounds and cuts, helped by the voluntary staff of the centre. Alice was there in her green WVS uniform, bathing a child's cut lip. Kay went over to her, feeling as if her insides were slowly righting themselves after a helter-skelter ride.

Alice looked up, amazed to see Kay, and Kay saw that she had been wounded too; there was blood oozing from a gash on her forehead and trickling along her eyebrow and down the side of her face.

"Mum, let me take over," Kay said.

"But you're hurt!" Alice exclaimed, and Kay realised that her own hands and clothes were stained with blood.

"No – someone I was helping. I haven't got a scratch. But shouldn't you get that cut seen to?"

"It can wait. Go and clean yourself up in the washroom round at the back," Alice said, "and then the most useful thing would be to get chairs for the people coming in, and wrap them in blankets for shock if they need them, and get them sweet tea from the trolley. Make sure the most urgent ones go straight to the nurses. Anyone really badly shocked can lie down on one of the beds in the classrooms. The blankets are in a box over there."

Kay was glad to have something useful to do. She washed her hands and set to work. She fetched chairs and rough brown blankets and tea, listened to the more talkative victims telling her over and over again what had happened to them, and removed the traumatised silent ones to a quiet room. From time to time she glanced across at her mother in admiration. Alice seemed to know instinctively how to treat each victim; some wanted to be cheerful and joke, others needed comfort or reassurance about relatives, some were hysterical and needed to be calmed. Kay felt herself flagging from tiredness and hunger, but Alice worked on regardless.

At last everyone had been tended to. Alice allowed one of the nurses to bathe and dress her own wound, which was not deep. Gradually the victims began to disperse. The worst cases were taken to hospital; others made their way home or were collected by relatives or friends. Only the greengrocer and his family remained to join the other temporary refugees at the centre; the flat above their shop was uninhabitable. The rest centre had no windows left, but it was a warm night and repairs could wait until the next day, although every room had to be swept clear of broken glass.

Kay and Alice stayed to share in the meal cooked by WVS volunteers, and only as they were leaving did Kay remember the bag of groceries she had put down somewhere in the street. It was still there; someone had thoughtfully stood the bag against a lamp post so that the contents should not spill out.

They went home and made a pot of tea and sat watching a hazy dusk fade to darkness, thinking about getting water heated for baths but too tired to make the effort. It had been a peculiar day, catastrophe dropping suddenly from a blue summer sky. In spite of her tiredness and anxiety, in spite of the distress of seeing people dead and wounded and terrified, in spite of knowing that the whole thing could happen again without warning, Kay felt curiously content. She felt that her mother shared her sense of quiet satisfaction in having worked together, doing what needed to be done.

LMF

*K*ay felt more reluctant than ever to leave her mother now that she had seen for herself what damage a flying-bomb could do. For a while, during that summer, the hated missiles came over daily. Kay worried incessantly, but at last the threat began to diminish as the advancing Allied troops gained ground in France and put the launching sites out of action. In August, the newspapers were full of triumphant pictures of the liberation of Paris. It was another big step towards the ending of the war.

Kay passed her ACW2 test and began to prepare for the next, which would qualify her as Leading Aircraftwoman. Now that she was Aircraftwoman First Class, her pay went up from fourteen to eighteen shillings a week. She had allocated half her pay to Alice at home, and was pleased to think of the extra money contributing to rent and household expenses. There was a certain pride, too, in mastering the technicalities of electronic theory and speeding up her Morse transmission, although she had begun to wonder what she would do with it all after the war. *After the war* had been a vague concept for months; it was strange to realise that it could actually come into existence.

Alistair continued to call in at the Flying Office to chat when Squadron Leader Roberts was not on duty. When he flew on ops, Kay could not help listening out specially for his voice asking for landing permission, and feeling relieved when his safe landing was chalked up on the board. Alistair was just a friend; he went out with several girls, including an attractive new WAAF officer who worked in Codes and Cyphers. Kay wanted no more than friendship, but all the same she was fond of him. Although losses on ops were not as frequent now as they had been during the last winter, those which did occur were still upsetting, and she did not want to be personally involved again. She wondered again about applying for a posting. Perhaps it was time for a change.

Alistair told her once that he had a conviction that he would survive the war.

"How can you say so?" she said, amazed.

Alistair said, "Statistically, I'm dead already. I've done more ops than a chap can expect to survive. Once I got past realising that, it didn't seem to matter so much. I stopped worrying about it. If it happens, it happens. But it won't."

Kay could not share his certainty. "Don't say it again. Even if you believe it, it's tempting fate to say it out loud."

"I don't go round telling everybody."

Kay wondered whether he could stick to his belief when he was up there in the bomber stream with the flak flying. Perhaps it gave him confidence, and confidence made him react fast and appropriately. Morale was an odd thing: she remembered a period during the spring when a certain accommodation hut was believed to be doomed, a whole succession of aircrew inhabiting it briefly before the effects officer came to clear out their belongings for the next arrivals. Superstitions grew easily on a bomber station.

In the early autumn, raids on German cities began again. Recent ops had concentrated on rocket bases and oil plants and on backing up the Allied advances, and Kay had hoped that the civilians of Germany would be left alone. Now Stettin and Darmstadt appeared on the battle order as targets. Guy Weldon, a flying officer Kay knew slightly, came up to the Control Office on the afternoon following the

Darmstadt raid, and told Kay that the whole town had been on fire.

"I'm sure they don't tell us the truth at briefing," he told her. "They said it was the centre for the enemy's chemical industry. You don't get modern chemical factories in the middle of country towns. I went to Darmstadt once, before the war – it's a beautiful old town. I mean it *was*—" He was obviously in distress. "And the target indicators were right over the centre. It must have been an inferno down there."

Squadron Leader Roberts had just come in from the main Operations Room with some document files, and Kay wondered whether he had overheard. When he told Guy Weldon sharply to stop hindering Kay in her work, she knew that he had.

What Guy had said disturbed Kay, reviving previous doubts. She thought of the flying-bomb in London and imagined what the effect would be when multiplied by the bomb load of over two hundred Lancasters, plus the devastating effects of incendiaries to add to the chaos and making rescue impossible.

Next day at lunch, Kay and Helen happened to be sitting at the same table as the bomb aimer from Guy Weldon's crew, who mentioned that they'd be getting a new pilot.

"Why?" Helen said.

"Skipper's gone LMF," the sergeant said. "Refused to fly on any more ops."

"LMF?" said Helen. "What's that?"

"Lack of Moral Fibre," Kay said, bitterly.

She had heard of aircrew going LMF on a few occasions, although it wasn't usually talked about much. It was a term used to denote an airman who wasn't up to the job, who had got the jitters, couldn't take it. She knew what would happen – Flying Officer Weldon would be stripped of his rank in a humiliating ceremony and removed swiftly from the station. He would never see the rest of his crew again in case he contaminated them. He would simply disappear.

"What will happen to him?" Helen said.

"Oh, he's gone already," the bomb aimer said. "He'll spend the rest of the war cleaning toilets, poor sod."

"But that's awful!" Helen said.

"It's not a great deal better than the last war," Kay said, "when shell-shocked cases were killed by firing squad. People aren't machines."

The bomb aimer shrugged. "There's a war on. He'll live, anyway. That's more than the rest of us can say."

The aircrews rarely spoke harshly of anyone who had "gone LMF"; they could understand only too well how the strain could become overwhelming. Officially, though, it was seen as a disgrace. And Kay thought that in this particular case it was not Lack of Moral Fibre, but possession of it, that had led to Flying Officer Weldon's decision.

She could not finish her meal. She wished she could have found Guy Weldon before he left, to say how appallingly she thought he had been treated. She wondered whether Squadron Leader Roberts had passed on what he had overheard in the Watch Office or whether Guy had made his stand of his own accord. Either way, no one would have been interested in his reasons; he had become, overnight, an embarrassing nuisance to be got rid of. It was a simple case of funk as far as Bomber Command was concerned.

She excused herself and went out to the airfield. The tractors were already taking the bomb loads out to the Lancasters for another raid tonight. The countryside looked autumnal, with yellowing grasses along the perimeter and thistledown drifting on a current of air; starlings chattered on the Flight Office roof. The giant bombers being prepared for war sat in the peaceful afternoon sunlight as if they were a natural part of the Lincolnshire scenery. It was a landscape Kay had grown to love, but she knew now that she must leave Windersby. She had delayed making the decision, but now it had made itself. She could not stay here and watch aircrew being sent off to another Darmstadt.

That same night she wrote off to apply for a posting to a training airfield. She spent a long time pondering her motives and the courses open to her. It would not be much of a gesture, whatever she did; no one would be any more interested in her reasons than they were in Guy Weldon's. She could not leave the WAAF, as she was now eighteen and old enough to be conscripted, and she could not suddenly become a conscientious objector, since she did not in principle object to the waging of war against Nazi Germany. And she knew that transferring to a non-operational unit was in effect not much different from working on a bomber station; it was simply moving herself a stage back from the front line. But she did not know what else to do.

Her posting came through fairly quickly: she was to go to Bardwell, a training unit in Northamptonshire. Alistair, who had recently come back from leave, asked her to go to Lincoln Cathedral with him before she left Windersby.

"I've never been there," he said. "Not inside."

"Never been in the cathedral? In all the time you've been here? But everyone goes there."

"Well, I haven't. You can tell me what to look at. I'm not very good at all that ecclesiastical stuff."

It was a mistake, as she realised as soon as she and Alistair entered the cool, dim interior. They gazed at the soaring arches of the fan vaulting and the jewelled windows, and then Kay could not stop herself from going over to the pulpit screen to look at the stone carvings. Among the fantastic creatures carved there, David had found a small human head, which he had said must be the stonemason – "making himself immortal. Doesn't he look as if he'd speak to you if he could?" Now the stonemason's presence was more solid than David's; he was still there, grinning at his medieval joke . . .

"Kay!" Alistair's voice broke into her thoughts, indignant. "You haven't listened to a word I've been saying!"

"Oh – sorry. Look at this." She showed him the carved head. "A little stone portrait. David said his expression is just like Charlie Fox's."

"It is, rather."

"He said he could imagine him getting everyone together for a sing-song when they knocked off work in the evening . . ."

When they went outside, Alistair said, "You know, if I wasn't such a thoroughly nice, generous-natured chap, I could really quite dislike David Evans."

"Whatever do you mean? Why should you?"

"Because I might stand a chance with you if he wasn't in the way."

Kay stared at him. "Don't joke like that!"

"I'm not joking. I mean it."

"But you— Just friends, you said!"

"I know. But that was then. This is now."

They had come to a standstill in the middle of the Cathedral Close. Alistair took her arm and for a moment she thought he was going to try to kiss her. She pulled away.

"Stop being silly, Alistair. I thought you knew—"

"I do know." He followed her through the Exchequergate. "But a chap can still hope. You will write to me when you get to Bardwell, won't you?"

"I don't know," Kay said. "I don't think it's a very good idea."

"Well, I'm going to write to you, anyway. Don't think you can get rid of me as easily as that, just by getting yourself posted away."

She had to laugh at this conceit. "It isn't because of you. Perhaps you're not as important as you think."

Alistair was never serious for long. "Don't be so obstinate, Kay. No other girl can resist my sunny personality or my overwhelming charm. Why should you think you can?"

"In that case, you needn't worry about being short of company," she said smoothly. "Now if you stop being such an idiot and talk about something else, I'll buy you a cup of tea before we go back."

Charlie and some of the others arranged a farewell party in the theatre, but it was a rather subdued occasion in spite of Charlie's lively renderings of music hall songs on the piano.

"I don't know how we're going to do the new show without you," Charlie said sadly.

"You'll find someone. Alistair says the new WAAF in the parachute section's always singing – you could get her to join in."

"It won't be the same."

Kay was sorry to let him down. The theatre group had been one of her main pleasures at Windersby, and Charlie in particular had always been kind to her.

She caught the first transport bus next morning without seeing anyone. The sadness of parting with friends was best not drawn out. It was a wet, squally day, rain lashing across the fields. The bus windows were steamed up and streaming with water, so that she could not even take a last look at the airfield. She felt as if she were leaving a large part of her life behind.

BARDWELL

Dear Mum,

Thanks for your letter – I'm glad things are quietening down again at the rest centre and that you've found somewhere for Mavis to live.

I've settled in here at Bardwell. It was pouring with rain when I got here, just like arriving at Windersby last summer – was that really only just over a year ago? It seems like a decade.

No more cosy rooms in pre-war quarters – it's back to a draughty old Nissen hut, sharing with thirteen others. No privacy except in the bath, though the water's never hot enough to stay there for long. And I've never found out why bath plugs are in such short supply in the RAF!

We're kept busy here, with training flights

day and night. The trainee crews don't stay here long before moving on to a heavy conversion unit, and then to operational squadrons. For each group that leaves, I hope the war will be over before they have to do the real thing. But it was awful news about the surrender at Arnhem, after the armies seemed to be moving on so quickly.

I hope you haven't seen anything of the new "flying gas main" rockets. One night when I was on watch I saw a bright green flash and then heard a deep roaring. It was only later when I read a description in the newspaper that I realised it must have been a V2 rocket. They sound terrifying.

The staff here are very pleasant, and I've made friends with a girl called Patsy who works in Meteorology . . .

Dear Kay,

Here I am at Blackpool, spud-bashing just as I expected. I shan't be able to look another potato in the eye (joke!) when I've finished here. Nearly every day I peel enough of the things to sink a battleship. Sometimes, as a special treat, I'm allowed to do the washing-up instead. You wouldn't recognise me in my overalls and apron and turban cap.

I'm in a billet with two other girls in a private house, with a landlady. She's quite a decent old *thing. Her two sons are in the army so she's quite pleased to have someone to look after. She gives us tea and toast when we come in and lets us sleep late on our day off. There are lots of RAF coming in and out of Blackpool on courses of various kinds, and there are concerts and dances to go to when we're off duty, so it's not so bad. But I wish it wasn't so cold and wet here, and I do miss the excitement of being on a bomber station! Oh, sorry, I suppose that's tactless. But I do feel quite nostalgic for the good old Windersby days. It's a bit cut off from it all over here in Blackpool.*

I'm sure you'll be pleased to hear that I'm not breaking the rules except in the very smallest respects.

Do write and tell me how you're getting on.

Love, Felicity

Dear Felicity,

I'm glad you're getting some fun along with the spud-bashing! I really can't imagine you in your cook's rig-out. I'm sure you manage to make it look the height of fashion. Will you try to change trades soon? It seems a great waste of your training otherwise.

I know what you mean about missing Windersby. Although it's very busy here, it's more a matter of routine – there isn't the sense of tension that used to grip the whole place before ops. But at least there aren't those awful blank spaces on the board. That's one of the things I certainly wasn't sorry to leave behind.

There is a lot of flying here. Bumps and circuits, blind approach training and cross country flights all day long, and then night flying practice too. We usually have to fill in the times on the board as well as doing the R/T and the log, so we have to jump up and down from the bench like grasshoppers.

Did you read about the sinking of the Tirpitz by Lancasters . . . ?

My dear Kay,

I know you have been waiting just as desperately as we have to hear something from the Air Ministry. At last something has come, but it is not good news, just a routine letter. The gist of it is that they are now assuming that David was killed, as there has been no news for so many months. I have copied out what the letter says, as I thought you would want to see it, even though of course is it not what any of us hoped for. It is as follows:

"Dear Mrs Evans, I am directed to inform you, with regret, that in view of the lapse of time and the absence of any further news regarding your son, Flight Sergeant D. Evans, since the date on which he was reported missing, the Air Council must regretfully conclude that *he lost his life, and his death has now been presumed, for official purposes, to have occurred on 24th March, 1944. The Council desire me to express to you and Mr Evans their deep and respectful sympathy."*

So there it is, nothing, after all this time.

The waiting has been dreadful but I think now we must all accept that David has gone, and comfort ourselves by thinking of him at peace and with God . . .

No! Kay wrote to her mother. *Not until every last prisoner comes home from Germany. I won't accept it. And if I did, I couldn't comfort myself the way Mrs Evans says – David didn't believe in God, and neither do I. If he is dead, then he is nowhere. But I won't believe it. It's not too late, not yet . . .*

And then she tore out the page and crumpled it up and threw it in the bin. The words she had just written were for herself, no one else. She clung to her hopes for David with silent tenacity; every day passed was a day closer to the end of the war (*surely* the end must be in sight, since the liberation of France), a shortening of her wait. She would not believe otherwise. David must be alive, somewhere, because . . . because what? Because she loved him, because she wanted him? But there was no logic to that. Every dead soldier, sailor, airman or

278

civilian was loved by somebody. Why should David be spared, when so many hundreds of thousands were dying? Logic was a hard frost, shrivelling her hopes; reason was a cold dispassionate voice, to which she tried to close her ears. David *must* be alive, somewhere.

Dear Kay,

Why didn't you answer my letter? I'm very disappointed in you. I didn't know you could be so hard-hearted.

As you see from the address, I'm no longer at Windersby. I've finished my second tour (you see, I was right) and I'm being posted to an OTU as an instructor. I hoped to end up at Bardwell, but no such luck – they're sending me up to North Yorkshire. Anyway, how are you? Not too bored, I hope, away from all the excitement.

I'm going to be spending a few days with a pal in Oxford before I go up to Yorkshire, so I hoped we might meet up. We could have a look at the old dreaming spires and punt down the river (even if it is winter) and do all the typical things one's supposed to do in Oxford. Could you get leave during the last week of November? Do say yes – I told you I wouldn't give up, and you can't hold out for ever.

Yours devotedly, Alistair.

Dear Alistair,

Congratulations on finishing your tour, and good luck with the instructing. I hear from the instructors here that it isn't as easy as people think! They use Wellingtons for training, but the instructors have all flown ops in Lancasters or Mosquitoes and they don't like the Wimpeys much — apparently they're not very tolerant of pilot error! The instructors have to be quick-witted and nippy with the dual controls. But I'm sure you'll be up to it.

It was nice of you to suggest meeting again, but no . . .

Dear Kay,

Thought you might like to hear from your old Windersby pals. Everything here's much the same as usual except that there's a bit of a gap where you used to be. We managed to put on the show in the end, after a lot of bother. We had a bit of luck when the new camp dentist turned out to be a good baritone. Sorry you missed it.

Alistair Tait has finished his tour and moved on (but perhaps you know that already). He's Flight Lieutenant now. The new crew that flies Easy nearly wrecked the old crate on their first op, and risked spoiling Sq. Ldr. Roberts's hairdo at the same time. The pilot took off so low that I thought he was going to take the

Watch Office roof with him. I'm sure there are skid marks along the viewing platform . . .

Dear Charlie,

Thanks for keeping in touch. It was good to hear the Windersby news and I'm glad you managed to do your concert. What are you doing next, a full-scale opera? I'm sure you'll end up on the London stage one day.

There has been the odd concert here, but not up to your standard. I haven't joined in any-thing – it wouldn't be as much fun as the Charlie Fox troupe.

The trainee aircrews come and go very quickly here. The people I know best are a nice girl called Patsy (who's in Meteorology, and engaged to a naval officer), the other Flying Control staff and the instructors.

Recently we had a group of trainees kept here for longer than usual because of bad weather, so it took them longer to get their flying hours in. While they were here, one of the instructors, a chap called Jock who lives with his wife in the village and is very popular with the crews, had his thirtieth birthday and they decided to play some jokes on him. You would have approved! They planned it all very carefully. Jock has a dog called Paddy, a lovely golden retriever, which he sometimes leaves tied up outside the Officers' Mess. While some of Jock's friends (who were in on the joke) were standing him birthday drinks, the trainees kidnapped Paddy and hid him in their hut. Then they replaced him with an enormous pig they'd "borrowed" from the next door farm. When Jock came out and saw the pig, he definitely thought he'd had a drink too many! The other instructors persuaded Jock to take the pig back to the farm – apparently pigs don't like to be led, so they all got tea trays from the mess and waved them at it. I wish I'd had a camera! Eventually they came back with pig manure all over their shiny shoes, only to find Paddy back outside the mess looking innocent!

Anyway, the trainees hadn't finished yet. Jock's got a little Fiat car which he's very proud of, and that night when he went to the Station HQ car park it had gone missing. We all pretended to search everywhere, knowing perfectly well that the trainees had lifted it to the flat roof of one of the Flight Offices. When they owned up, one of them said, "It was for your own good, sir. We thought you were a bit the worse for wear after all that drinking, and shouldn't drive home. We heard you'd been chasing around after imaginary pigs." Now everyone makes oinking noises whenever Jock appears!

It's just as well that life in Bomber Command has its lighter side sometimes.

I do miss Windersby, even though I wanted

*to leave. It has a lot of happy memories for me
as well as the awful ones . . .*

Dear Kay,

    *You won't believe this, but I'm getting mar-
ried! I know it's sudden, but I never did do
things by halves.*

    *His name's Frank and he's an instructor in
the Radio School here at Blackpool. No more
aircrew for me! I met him at a dance and
we've had quite a whirlwind romance. I think
you'd approve. He's twenty-nine, old enough
to be sensible (just what I need), and we're
going to get married as soon as the war ends.
We're going to live in Carlisle, where he comes
from. I hope you'll come to the wedding. I've
even written home to tell my parents but
they'll probably think I'm marrying beneath
me and won't bother to reply. Anyway, I don't
care.*

    *You see, I'm turning out quite respectable
after all . . .*

Dear Mum,

    *I'm sorry I didn't get home at all over the
Christmas period. I could have had a 48-hour
pass for New Year but I'm sure you'll understand that I wanted it to be as unlike last year as
possible. I thought it would be better to save up
the leave and have it later. Anyway, I'm glad*

you spent Christmas with Lorna. You must have had such a lot to talk about after all this time.

Happy New Year, and good riddance to 1944 . . .

V.E. DAY

Stratford-upon-Avon was full of off-duty servicemen and women. They crowded every tea shop, strolled along the pavement and riverside and looked at the notices outside the theatre. Kay and Patsy, there for the day, threw crumbs from their sandwiches to the ducks on the canal basin and watched a coal barge negotiating the lock gates. A chilly wind was blowing off the river, ruffling the water. Across the basin, the new Shakespeare Theatre was a functional red-brick building, not unlike pre-war airfield accommodation – not quite what Kay had been expecting. She and Patsy had tickets to see *Much Ado About Nothing* later on. The other plays for the season were *Twelfth Night* and *The Merry Wives of Windsor*. All comedies; no tragedies for wartime. She remembered that this time last year she had been rehearsing *A Midsummer Night's Dream*. If only life could be resolved as happily as a Shakespeare comedy.

"I wonder what we'll be doing a year from now?" she said.

"I shall be married, I hope," Patsy said. "We're going to arrange it as soon as the war ends. We'll be married whenever Robert can get leave and he'll apply for a regular posting."

"So you're going to be a proper navy wife? Won't you be lonely?"

"It depends where Robert goes," Patsy said. "If he gets a permanent posting overseas I might be able to go with him. I applied once to go abroad with the WAAF, but they wouldn't let only daughters go because of the risk."

"They don't mind about only sons putting themselves at risk," Kay said. "Why should daughters be treated differently? Why is it only acceptable for men to fight wars and die?"

"You don't mean you'd have wanted to fight?" Patsy said. "I wouldn't."

"No, of course not," Kay said, watching the milling ducks. "But it's like a kind of safety valve, isn't it, keeping wars for men? If men do the fighting while women support them, it seems heroic and brave. If women fought too, then it would seem normal, and that would be more frightening . . ."

The pieces of crust were all gone. She shook the paper bag over the water and the ducks surged forward for the last few crumbs, then gradually swam off towards a group of American airmen who were unwrapping sandwiches.

"At least we can *think* about the war ending now," Patsy said. "It hasn't always seemed much of a prospect."

"Yes. But I wonder what sort of world will be left. There seems no limit to the horrible things people can do to each other."

"You mean because of Auschwitz? The death camp?"

"Partly that," Kay said.

They had read about it in the newspapers, the Russians reaching Auschwitz. Kay couldn't forget the nightmare photographs of the still living: skull-like faces, skin stretched like aged parchment over stick limbs. It reminded her of medieval paintings of hell, with bodies being forked into the flames. But this wasn't some medieval painter's vision of hell. It was real; it was happening now. People could let it happen, guards could watch their prisoners become living skeletons and could herd them off to be shot and gassed. And soon afterwards Kay had been equally distressed by the bombing of

Dresden, which had resulted in a massive fire-storm and the loss of life on a scale which she could not begin to comprehend. She hated to think of the courageous airmen she had known setting out on such a mission.

She still found the subject hard to discuss. If she criticised the deliberate bombing of civilians, was she in effect saying that everyone in the air force, herself included, was misguided? Would she be saying that David and all the other thousands had risked and lost their lives for the wrong reasons? The tactical bombing raids had certainly contributed to the defeat of Germany, but did it follow that anything was permissible which could hasten that defeat?

She thought of what Guy Weldon had said about Darmstadt. It was impossible for an ordinary person to know the truth behind the official statements and the newspaper reports, but she felt strongly that if the aircrews were being misled about the nature of their targets, it was a betrayal of the ideals they were fighting for.

Kay was idly looking over a list of names of student aircrew when the name P/O Evans, D. jumped out at her. She held the sheet for Jock to see, and pointed to the name. "Pilot Officer D. Evans – do you know what his first name is?"

Jock thought for a moment, drawing on his pipe.

"Er . . . Douggie, I think they call him. Nice enough lad. A bit too impulsive sometimes. Why, do you know him?"

"No," Kay said. "I know another D. Evans, that's all."

David would have been Pilot Officer by now, perhaps Flying Officer. She could hear his voice, saying, "I thought it would be easier to get married on an officer's pay." She could see him standing there in the windy field, his hurt expression, the scene she had played over and over in her mind without being able to change a word she had said.

Evans was a common enough name, but seeing it typed there on a list of new crews made it seem as if David's name was like an aircraft code letter, transferable to a new owner.

At last there was a real prospect that the aircrew Kay guided down to their landings would never see operations. As the days lengthened into spring, the newspaper front pages were splashed with headlines announcing the latest advances. The Allies were crossing the Rhine, reaching the Ruhr; the Allied and Russian front lines were closing around Berlin. In April, while the hedgerows and woods of Northamptonshire flourished new growth in an exceptionally warm spring, the Belsen and Buchenwald death camps were opened up, with new reports of atrocities.

The horrors and the astonishments came so fast that it was difficult to take in each new item. Previously larger events had caused only passing comment on camp, but now everyone wanted to listen to the radio or snatch a glimpse of the newspaper. Fact mingled with rumour as the latest hot topic was passed around the mess or the Flying Control Office. When news came that Hitler and Eva Braun had shot themselves, Kay felt stunned; it seemed impossible. Surely, now, the end could not be far away.

She was due to go home for two days' leave on Tuesday. On Monday evening she packed her bag and went to bed early, ready to get up in time for the first transport to London. She was awoken abruptly by the loud clanging of a bell. Her first thought was that it was an air raid: why else would a bell be ringing in the middle of the night? The other girls were stirring, mumbling, some pulling clothes on. Kay couldn't think what was happening, but supposed she ought to get up and see.

The door banged open and a WAAF bounded in and turned all the lights on. "Get up, everyone!" she yelled. "The war's over! It's all over!"

Outside, people were emerging sleepily in

dressing-gowns and pyjamas and parts of uniform, some still under the impression that
there was an emergency. Someone shouted,
"It's true! We heard it on the midnight news –
the war's over, Germany's surrendered!"

Excitement, bafflement and disbelief registered on the surrounding faces. Officers came
out to see what all the fuss was about and
heard the news for themselves. The NAAFI
and the messes were opened up and someone
rushed into a hut for a gramophone to play at
full volume, soon competing with the piano
and a trumpet from the Sergeants' Mess. The
NAAFI staff served beer and cocoa and soon
the area between the huts was one big party,
with all the lights turned on. People were
dancing wildly on the grass and even the station commander was polkaing energetically
with one of the WAAF cooks, while Kay
found herself swept along in a conga, weaving
in and out of all the abandoned beds in the
huts. She began to think she must be
hallucinating. Could it really be true, the war
was over?

At about three in the morning the party died
down and Kay went back to bed, although
everyone in the hut chattered excitedly for the
rest of the night. She got up in time for an
early breakfast. In the cookhouse she found
the staff from the Flying Control Office who

had been on duty since midnight and had missed the celebrations.

"A phone message came for you a while ago," the corporal said. "Some bloke. I couldn't make head nor tail what he was on about but I wrote it down just as he said and put it on the WAAF notice board."

"What was his name?" Kay said quickly.

The corporal shook his head with maddening, ponderous slowness. "Can't remember now. Something to do with Windersby, I think he said."

Kay left the cookhouse, her heart pounding as she crossed the interminable distance to the Waafery. It couldn't be, it *couldn't* . . .

The folded slip of paper was on the WAAF notice board, with ACW Leary pencilled on it. Kay took it down with trembling fingers and fumbled to open it. The writing blurred in front of her eyes as she tried to take it all in at once.

The corporal's childish handwriting read: *If you're not still involved in piggy business, come down to London and meet us at Charing Cross Station. Six p.m., main clock. Charlie.*

She leaned against the wall, refolding the note. How could she have been so stupid as to to think, even for a moment . . . Things didn't happen like that. She felt like weeping with disappointment, drained of the ridiculous hope of the last two minutes. But then she opened the note and re-read Charlie's message and thought, well, why not? It is a special day, after all. The first day of peacetime.

At Charing Cross Kay wondered how she was ever going to find Charlie. The streets were swarming with people; the day had been declared a national holiday and the capital resembled a vast party, like the night-time one of a few hours ago multiplied a thousandfold. Union Jacks and bunting and Victory banners were draped from windows, and people were milling about in silly hats and dancing in the streets. The station was dense with passengers pouring off the trains or queuing to get on them: civilians, nurses, soldiers and airmen in every variety of uniform, sailors lugging kitbags through the crowd.

Kay pushed her way slowly through the packed mass towards the main clock. Noisy greetings and farewells were taking place all around her but there was no sign of Charlie. Meet us at Charing Cross, his message had said; she wondered who else he had meant. She tried to stand in one place beneath the clock but was buffeted to and fro by passing bodies. It was hopeless trying to see over the jostling heads, she was far too short, but she craned her neck and stood on tiptoe. If she could not find him, she would return home and go to the party put on by Alice and others of the WVS at the rest centre . . .

"Kay! Kay!"

A hand stretched up, waving, and suddenly she glimpsed Charlie's beaming face and foxy hair. He pushed his way towards her and hugged her vigorously, lifting her right off her feet.

"You made it! I didn't know if you'd be able to get off."

"I had leave – I'm staying at my mother's."

"Come on. Let's get out of this crush." He took her hand and pulled her through the fore-court towards the front entrance, by the Charing Cross Hotel. "The others are here some-where . . . We all got a bus down. There they are . . ."

Kay waved, seeing Joyce and Helen and some of the others. They all exchanged hugs and greetings, and began to make their way slowly down the Strand towards Trafalgar Square. The bells of St-Martin-in-the-Fields rang out in a continuous joyful pealing. Joyce started to tell Kay a complicated story about the journey which Kay could follow only in snatches; it was difficult to keep together in the surging, swelling crowd. Everyone seemed to be going in the same direction, in some un-spoken common purpose. Pubs had their doors open to the street and every restaurant and café was bursting; someone had climbed a lamp post and was waving drunkenly from the spar. It seemed that every Londoner had come out to join in the celebrations or to hear Winston Churchill addressing the crowds earlier in the day. Everyone had gone mad; musicians played in Trafalgar Square and people were dancing and kissing complete strangers and splashing about in the fountains. It was a warm, sultry evening with sunshine breaking through low thundercloud, but no threat of rain or storm could dampen the jubilant spirits of the crowd. After a while Kay and Charlie and the others went to sit on the steps of the National Gallery to look on. As dusk fell, every building was lit up and every streetlamp shone; searchlights performed a victory dance in the sky while ships' sirens blared from the Thames.

Kay watched, fascinated. It all seemed unreal; she felt detached from the mood of euphoria. Not everyone was revelling. Here and there, on the edge of the crowd, was a face expressing bewilderment or exhaustion or utter grief. Kay thought of the uncountable losses, the countless thousands upon thousands of lives destroyed in Warsaw and Leningrad, Buchenwald and Auschwitz, and here in London, and in Dresden and Darmstadt and at sea and in the desert. The war had picked up human lives and destinies like dried leaves in a whirlwind, destroying and scattering them, leaving tattered remains where the eddies of fortune had dropped them. It was impossible to believe that she or any other individual could matter very much, seen in such a perspective.

"What will you do now, Charlie?" she asked.

"When I'm demobbed, you mean? I'll stay on in aviation, I reckon. Passenger aircraft. Demob's not going to come tomorrow, though. There's still the war going on in Japan."

"What will Windersby be doing from now on?"

"Mercy flights," Charlie said, "Spam trips, they call them. Dropping food parcels and clothing in Holland, and fetching troops back from Italy."

Kay liked that: the war planes turning to bringers of comfort.

Charlie leaned back on his elbows against the National Gallery steps and looked up at the searchlight beams playing on the underside of the clouds. "What about you? After demob?"

"I don't know."

"You'll get married, I bet," Charlie said, turning to look at her. "Some lucky bloke."

"No, I won't."

She nearly added, from habit, "Not unless—" but she did not. Miracles did occur, but she knew suddenly that her own personal miracle was not going to happen. This morning had been the last flicker of hope. Whatever kind of life she might plan for herself could not include David. He had gone, irrevocably, where her thoughts could not follow him. Had he died for this, or for nothing? She still did not know.

Tomorrow the revelry would be over, and the dancers and musicians and flag wavers would go back to their jobs. The rebuilding would begin, the dead would be mourned. Life would carry on, peacetime life.

"I can't think of this as victory," she said to Charlie. "It's just an ending."

EPILOGUE: TAMSIN

Tamsin squinted into the bright sunlight at the Lancaster flying low over the runway, flanked by a Spitfire and a Hurricane: the Battle of Britain Flight. Dozens of camcorders filmed the fly-past for fathers or grandfathers who had flown the planes or for relatives who wanted to remember. In the VIP enclosure were men and women who must have been here in the war, perhaps people Nan had known; they had probably come especially to see this particular programme item. After the hi-tech of the previous displays, the three war planes were gallant survivors of an earlier age.

Tamsin listened to the drone of the Lancaster engines as it did its solo display and thought how familiar that sound must have been to Nan, watching the planes take off night after night, waiting for them to come back. Perhaps that squarish brick building was the wartime control office in which she had sat, that night the particular plane she was listening for hadn't come back. How often that must have happened here, in nearly six years of war . . .

Jim had finished a roll of film. Winding it back, he said, "Your grandad didn't fly bombers, did he?"

"No," Tamsin said. "He was ground crew, an engineer. Ground crew and entertainment manager, Nan said. He was always putting on plays and concerts, getting everyone organised. She said he should have worked as a Butlins Redcoat afterwards."

"Did they get married while they were here?"

They sat down on the warm grass to wait for the next stage of the display, and Jim took a new film out of his pocket.

"No, not till a year or two after the war. Nan went out to Essen, on her own, to work with the rehabilitation of the German people. She said it was absolutely devastating, the damage: people living in cellars, just existing, with nothing. Far worse than the Blitz in London. That's what made her join CND later, that and the atom bomb."

"Brave of her to go out there alone."

"Yes. And later on Grandad went out there too, and then they came back to get married."

Tamsin gazed out over the expanse of the airfield, in the direction of the coast. Jim followed her gaze, and she said, "So if the other one I was telling you about – the aircrew one – hadn't got killed, she'd have married him instead, and I wouldn't be here now."

"No. But then everyone's life is like that. We're all just a random collection of chances. One thing happens rather than another."

"I suppose so." Tamsin took her hat off and lay on her back and looked up at the sky. Of course she knew there was no reason behind it, no pattern. But she liked to imagine that there *were* patterns, all the same.

"And then I suppose you could say the same thing about your mum," Jim said. "If she hadn't—"

"Oh well, *Mum*." Tamsin closed her eyes against the sun's glare. "It's really quite incredible that I'm here at all, isn't it?"

Jim wound his new film on and pressed the shutter. Hearing the click, she opened her eyes and saw the camera pointing at her.

"What was that for?"

"Photographic evidence that you definitely are here," he said, and then, "I bet there's a memorial plaque somewhere, with all the names of the missing airmen on it. That other guy would be listed on it, the one who died. I wonder if it's here, or in the church in the village?"

Tamsin propped herself on one elbow. She was pleased by his interest. "There must be one somewhere. I never thought of that." She looked out across the runway and said, "Out there, on the airfield, was where she saw him off for the last time. She told me, she said 'Good luck,' and he said, 'See you tomorrow,' and got into his plane, and that was the last she ever saw or heard of him. She had a gold locket that he gave her for Christmas and that was all she had left. She never knew what happened – the wreckage of the plane was never found, not even after the war. Isn't that awful?" Tears prickled her eyes as she thought of that long-ago parting.

"But he'll be on the plaque, all the same."

"Yes, we can go and find him," Tamsin said, liking the idea. But then a thought struck her. "No, we can't. We don't know who he was. David, but I'm sure Nan never told me his last name. He was Welsh, she said."

"Lloyd, Jones, Thomas, Evans, Rees?" Jim guessed.

Parachutists overhead were streaking the sky with coloured smoke trails, but the past was more absorbing.

"There must be hundreds of names on that plaque," Tamsin said. "We'd never know which one he was. But I've got something else."

She reached into her shoulder bag and unfastened her purse and held out what it contained in the palm of her hand for Jim to see.

"The locket!" He leaned closer. "She left it to you?"

Tamsin nodded. They both looked closely at the gold locket and chain. The chain was tarnished and dull. The edges of the heart-shaped locket bore traces of a chased design, but the rest was smooth and shiny with wear.

"You didn't tell me," Jim said.

"No . . . She and Grandad were happy together, but she kept this. She always wore it."

"It must have been a bit odd for your grandad," Jim said, "knowing that she'd have married the other bloke, if he hadn't died."

"Mmm. But that must have happened to a lot of people in wartime. It was Grandad who told me about it first, about Nan and David, when I wanted to know what it was like in the war. And then I asked Nan and she talked about it too. I think that's why she left me the locket, because she'd been telling me about him, just before . . . I keep thinking of all the other things I should have asked her. It's too late now."

Jim took the locket and turned it over in his hand. "Does it open up? Is there anything inside?" he suggested. "People used to put photos in them."

"No, look." Tamsin took it back and probed at the catch with her thumbnail. The locket sprang open and she held it carefully to show Jim. "Not a photo, but this."

In the heart-shaped cavity was a coil of hair, dark and glossy.

"His?" Jim said.

Tamsin nodded. "Isn't that strange? Nobody knows where he ended up, but this little piece of hair has survived all that time."

She clicked the locket closed again and held it up so that it revolved slowly on its chain, catching and reflecting the sunlight.

"Are you going to wear it?" Jim said.

"I don't think so."

It was more than just a piece of jewellery to be casually worn; she did not want to risk losing it. It was a small token of that wartime love story which had ended like so many others in sadness and loss. But Nan had kept the locket, and her memories. Who could say that it had all been loss, after all?